I0530678

Shopping for a Groom

Book 1 in the Brides of Seattle series

By Kathleen Sprout

Proverb Press

DEDICATION

To my Lord Jesus who has given me all I have, and my friends, Keith, Judy, Lavada and Sally who have prayed for me and encouraged me on my writing journey, and my amazing family who laughs in all the right places

CHAPTER ONE

"She can't stay here, Ginger."

"SHHH! She'll hear you."

The man's response was too low for Marta to hear from her position behind the bathroom door. She'd just stepped out of the shower and thrown on an ankle-length plaid flannel robe she found hanging on a hook behind the door. Suddenly shivering, she clenched her fists. She wanted to storm into the living room where her best friend and that tyrant were arguing. And over her! This was the last thing she expected after the warm welcome Ginger gave her just an hour before when she'd gotten off the bus with her meager belongings. Who was he to be telling her friend what to do, anyway? A boyfriend? The landlord?

And what did he mean, she couldn't stay there? She needed to straighten this guy out. It wasn't like she could just pick up and leave. After spending most of her money on the bus ticket from Portland, a month's rental for a room in her friend's apartment, Marta barely had enough left to help Ginger out with groceries. Besides, where would she go? She didn't know anyone else in Seattle.

Marta quickly grabbed a bath towel and wrapped it around her wet head, tucking the ends in to secure it. Putting her ear to the door, she listened for voices. Could she make it from the bathroom to the bedroom and her clothes without being seen? She could no longer hear anyone and decided to make a run for it. Going toe-to-toe with a strange man required she at least be dressed. She slowly opened the door and peeked out. Good. They'd gone. She ran for Ginger's spare bedroom and skidded to a stop at the door when she saw who was inside.

"Yes?"

Marta clutched the robe to her chest and glared at the man whose sarcasm only elevated her resolve. The nerve! She stood as straight as she could and spoke with her best Grace Kelly hauteur.

"It never occurred to me I'd find a stranger in my own room."

Mr. Rude raised a dark eyebrow, lifted her ratty old duffle bag from the bed and set it on the floor between them. Not appearing the least bit cowered by the fact she'd caught him trespassing in her room, he turned and began pulling clothes, men's clothes, from one of several boxes stacked next to the bed.

"Look, I'm sorry," he said, as he placed several perfectly folded sweatshirts in a dresser drawer. "This is not your room. This is my apartment and therefore my room. Why don't you go back to the bathroom and get dressed? Ginger is calling the women's shelter and when I get done here, I'll drive you down there."

"The women's shelter?" Marta could barely squeak the words out. Barefoot, wearing nothing but a borrowed robe, and conscious of the towel slipping from her head, she felt less and less like the Princess of Monaco. She felt like . . . a bag lady; an unwanted, unworthy human being who could be tossed aside as easily as yesterday's newspaper. But that was in the past. Things were going to be different now. Nobody was going to treat her like dirt. Ever again. This move to a new city was supposed to be a new start. A little thing like a strange man in her room was not going to get in her way.

"I'm afraid you've got it wrong, mister. Ginger invited me to stay here and she rented this room to me. Now if you don't get out of here right now, I'm going to start screaming my head off! Hopefully someone will call the police and you can explain to them what you're doing here."

Marta flinched as the man took a step toward her, but stood her ground. He was taller than her, but not much. He couldn't be over six feet tall. She nearly wavered when his startling blue eyes met hers, and then slowly lowered his gaze to her bare feet. She thought she detected a flash of amusement spark in his eyes but it was quickly replaced by his deadpan stare as he once again raised his gaze back to her face.

"Your toes are curled."

"What?"

Your toes are curled. I don't think you're as tough as you pretend."

"Ginger! GIN---GERRR! Get in here!" Marta didn't take her eyes off Mr. Total Uncaring Arrogant Meanie, as she rapidly renamed him, till she heard her friend burst down the hall behind her.

She saw immediately that Ginger had been crying. Streaks of navy blue mascara mingled with the peach colored rouge on her cheeks. Marta knew her friend could turn on the tears at the drop of a hat, but this time she could sympathize. Tears threatened to weaken her defense against this stranger.

"Please tell your friend, or landlord, or whoever this is, to kindly vacate my room."

"Oh, Martha, this is all my fault." Ginger sniffed, pausing to give the man a pitiful look she'd perfected in junior high. "I forgot to tell my brother you were coming and I didn't know he was moving back in."

Marta looked from her friend to the dark haired man standing with his arms crossed. Her brother? They weren't a bit alike. Ginger was short, her face was covered with streaked makeup and she was one of the sweetest people Marta knew. He was tall, had five o'clock shadow on his stony face, and was mean as a snake. "Your brother? You finally found him?"

"Well, it's more like he found me. I guess I should introduce you two. Martha, this is my brother, Josh."

"Marta. I go by Marta, now."

"When did you change your name? I like the name, 'Martha'."

Marta narrowed her eyes. "Wasn't he supposed to be in jail or something?"

"Oh Martha," Ginger giggled, "That was years and years ago. And it wasn't jail; it was juvie."

Marta turned and glared at Ginger's formerly missing brother. Too bad he hadn't stayed that way. "What was he in for, breaking and entering?"

Pointedly ignoring Marta's remark, Josh slammed a drawer shut and said "If you two ladies would stop yammering and get out of here, I could finish so we could find a place for Miss . . . whatever to stay."

Marta spoke up, "I'm staying right here. I paid Ginger an entire month's rent."

Josh scooped up another stack of flawlessly folded T-shirts and spoke in an exasperated voice. "This is *my* apartment. Ginger is subletting from me. Give her back her money, Ginger. I told you she couldn't stay here. I've told you dozens of times it isn't safe to keep bringing strangers home with you."

"I can't. I spent it. And she's not a stranger. I've known her for ages and ages."

"Then she can sleep on the couch, or bunk in with you. I have an early appointment in the morning and have to get some sleep."

"Martha, er I mean Marta, you're welcome to share my room. You can have the bed and I'll pull out the cot I got at a garage sale last week."

Marta shivered as a trickle of cold water escaped from her turban and drizzled down her neck. Bunking with Ginger in the same apartment as an ex con? Was there another choice? She didn't even have any clean or decent clothes to put on, thanks to some stupid bus driver who managed to lose her suitcase during the three-hour trip from Portland. At least there was an oversize T-shirt in her duffle bag. She could sleep in that while her clothes were in the washing machine. The bag's other items wouldn't be half as useful, but Marta hadn't planned on living out of it. Her

4

down pillow, which had been a gift from her former employer, a New Testament, also a gift, and a week's supply of chocolate bars . . . things she thought she might need on the journey and were all the possessions she now had.

It suddenly dawned on her that the very robe she was wearing probably belonged to Ginger's brother as well. Marta bent and retrieved her bag with as much dignity as her attire would afford. "It is rather late. I suppose it would be ok for one night, Ginger. However, I wouldn't want to crowd you, so tomorrow we'd better figure out other arrangements for your brother." She left the room without even glancing toward the man who could ruin all her plans.

***

Marta waited till she heard Josh leave for work the next morning before leaving Ginger's bedroom to join her for breakfast. After her friend said grace over the breakfast, she munched on the sugar-coated cereal and silently vowed she'd offer to take over the grocery shopping.

"I'm sorry my brother was so rude last night. He is pretty overprotective but I don't complain too much 'cause he's done so much for me. Put me in this apartment. Helped me find a reliable used car. Oh, he's a little old fashioned in his ideas . . . more like a doting dad than a brother."

"Why does he want to live with you? Most men his age value their privacy and independence."

"I think he just wants to be close by in case I need him. He doesn't live here all the time, you know. He lives in the various vacant apartments while he's fixing them up and then moves out when they're ready to rent." Ginger's eyes filled with pride as she spoke of her brother.

"Well, I see you two have grown close, but three people in this tiny apartment make it pretty crowded. As soon as I find a good job, and a steady income, I'll be looking for a place of my own. The sooner the better, too."

"There's no hurry to find a job. I'm not going to let you starve, Marta. You mean too much to me. Why don't you sign up for beauty school? When you graduate, we could work together . . . maybe even open our own shop someday?"

Marta lowered the classified section of the Seattle Times she'd purchased at the bus station and looked at her childhood friend. Ginger's hair stuck out from her head in maroon spikes. Her bright blue nail polish and heavy makeup shouted a similar fashion statement. Marta's affection for her friend prevented her from saying the words that would surely hurt her feelings. However, there was no way she intended on spending *her* life wearing one faddish hairstyle after another. No, not Martha Ellen Patrosky. People were going to look at her with respect and maybe even envy. Maybe she should change her last name too. No. Too expensive. She'd probably have to get an attorney and go to court to do it. She would have a new last name once she was married anyway.

"I don't think I'd be very good at doing people's hair, Ginger."

"Sure ya would. You just need to stretch yourself a little. For starters, you need to get rid of that boring hairstyle. It's way too long. Let me cut it and give you a perm-"

"No!" The last thing Marta wanted was Ginger's anxious fingers digging around in her hair. No telling what she would end up looking like. A punk rocker. Or worse. She had to take control. "Ginger," she gently said. "It's not that I don't appreciate you letting me temporarily stay here. I've loved seeing you after all this time. I just don't see myself spending my life working at a job where I'll have to stand on my feet all day."

Regrettably, Marta saw Ginger's face fall. She hoped this wasn't a precursor to the tears her friend so easily dissolved into when they were both youngsters living together in a foster home. Why couldn't she see there was more to life than spending it washing other people's hair? From what she's heard, the pay was terrible and the customers were impossible to please. Marta was never going

6

to fall in the trap of working for nothing again. She'd spent most of her childhood taking care of kids for her numerous foster parents. Doing the chores that nobody else wanted to do. Even after she reached the magic age of eighteen and left the foster care system, the only job she could find, after a long period of living on the streets, was caring for a sick and dying woman. Now at almost twenty-four, it was time to get on with the life she dreamed of.

"You're no better than me, Marta," Ginger sniffed. "We come from the same place. How come you're so hoity-toity all of a sudden?"

"Of course I don't think I'm better than you. You're my best friend and always will be. But, I've had a chance to see how the other half lives, Ginger. And I liked it. You would too."

"Not if it means acting like a phony. Not if it meant turning my back on my friends."

"I'm not turning my back on you, Ginger. I simply expressed that I don't have the inclination to work in the personal care field."

"See! You can't even talk like a regular person anymore. All those big words you use. Why can't you just be fun, like you used to be?"

Marta sighed. Ginger didn't understand. It wasn't her fault, either. She'd never been exposed to the nice things in life; hadn't lived in a mansion in Portland Heights. If she had, she would tear down that awful velvet painting of the bullfighter that threatened to fall off the wall above the old tattered couch. Even though it was probably the most expensive thing in the room, it still offended Marta's eyes when she looked at it. "There's nothing wrong with a person trying to better themselves, Ginger. Do you want to end up on welfare with a bunch of hungry kids like your sister?"

"I'm not on welfare and I never will be. I work hard, go to church, do volunteer work and I'm a good person." Ginger wiped some crumbs from the table as if to prove her point. "So what are you planning to do?"

"I'm going to find a job . . . a good job, maybe in a prestigious office. Some place where people will treat me with respect. Maybe I can even find a rich husband."

"You're going to marry for money? You can't do that! It's obscene. I don't think it's even Christian."

"Haven't you heard that God helps those who help themselves? I'm taking control of my own destiny, that's all. It's not like I'd steal some man's heart and money and then run. When I marry, it will be forever. Only I plan on marrying someone who can take care of me."

"Don't you know that the Lord supplies all our needs? Have you forgotten you placed your life in His hands when we were in High school? You'd better not tell Josh what your plans are. He'll kick you out of here for sure."

"She'd 'better not tell Josh' what?"

Marta snapped her head around and cringed under Josh's menacing stare. When had he come back? Her throat went dry at the prospect of being out on the street again.

"I was just about to tell her you didn't allow any pets in the building." Ginger stammered. "Like a cat. You know, going over the apartment rules with her." Her voice trailed off.

"A cat?" Josh's tone suggested he didn't buy that explanation for a second.

"Marta's always loved animals. Why wouldn't she want a sweet little kitty now that she's got a home here with us?"

Josh poured himself a cup of coffee and glowered at the two women. What kind of kook had his sister drug home this time? And what was she really up to? It was obvious from her appearance she'd been living on the street. He wished Ginger would confine her generosity to volunteering in the women's shelter instead of dragging people home who would only take advantage of her. It wasn't as if she had a lot to share. His sister was just getting on her feet herself. He took a sip of coffee and grimaced in distaste.

"Ginny, won't you ever learn to brew a decent pot of coffee? And you . . ." He gestured toward Marta with his cup, "A cat is out of the question. You'd better concentrate on getting a job and finding a place to live."

"I assure you, I have no intention of staying here any longer than necessary." Marta's voice was low, but filled with resolve. "As you can see, I'm looking through the want ads now."

Josh glanced at the classified section next to Marta's half eaten bowl of cereal. He had to give her credit. She had circled several ads. Maybe she was serious. He reached across the table to pick up the paper.

"Maybe I c-"

"That's my paper!" Marta yanked the pages away from him.

"I was merely going to offer to help. What kind of job are you looking for? What are your qualifications?"

"I don't need any help, thank you." She folded the paper, hiding the section she'd marked.

He wondered what she was hiding besides the help wanted section. Well, at least the ads shouldn't lead to anything illegal or immoral. He took a good look at her. A woman with her looks could easily get into trouble. He sent up a silent prayer that this latest stranger wouldn't get his sister involved in anything risky. After years of having no parents or home of their own, they were finally getting their lives established and had both joined a nearby community church. Things would be good for him and his sister . . . if only she would use a little discernment in her choice of friends.

"Ginny, I came back to remind you I'm driving you to work this morning."

Ginger pouted, "I was going to have Marta do it so she could have my car to job hunt."

Josh scowled. Would she ever learn to be more responsible? "Ginger. Don't you remember? I made an appointment two weeks ago to get your car serviced."

"Oh. I guess I forgot."

"I can take the bus, Ginger. In fact, I'd rather do that than take a chance of getting myself lost in a strange city," Marta said.

"See? Your friend here can get along just fine. Now get your purse and let's get going or we're going to be late." He looked at Marta, relieved she hadn't jumped at the opportunity to get her hands on Ginger's car. No telling what condition she would have returned it in. If she returned it at all. He tightened his jaw. Ginger was way too trusting.

"I'll be back soon to check on you," he said meaningfully to Marta as he opened the door and left.

***

Marta decided not to spend any more time going through the want ads. If she was going to find a job and get away from Ginger's arrogant brother, she'd better start going on interviews right away. He'd practically insinuated she was going to steal something if left alone in the apartment. How did Ginger stand such an overbearing tyrant running her life? She'd have to have a talk with her tonight. Ginger didn't need a caretaker at her age.

The most promising ad she'd circled asked for a receptionist at a racquet club. She could handle that. Plus, a lot of professional men spent every lunch hour at those places. It wasn't her first choice for a job, but she couldn't very well apply for a position in a fancy office in the clothes she'd worn on the bus. Her jeans and top would have to do for this interview. She hoped they weren't expecting skinny, hard-body, applicants wearing spandex. She'd be out of luck on all counts.

Marta lifted her sneakers and frowned at the scuffmarks. Padding on her bare feet to the kitchen sink, she scrubbed her shoes with a paper towel and kitchen cleanser. The paper towel dissolved before she could see a difference. She needed a brush. Not finding one under the sink, she walked down the hall to the bathroom. Nothing under that sink or in the cupboards either. What did Ginger use to

10

clean with, anyway? The only thing in the apartment that came close was a toothbrush. One of those battery operated ones. Would she dare borrow it? If she replaced the brush part while she was out, no one would know. *Desperate times calls for desperate measures.* All she had to do was get back before anyone else.

Marta returned to the kitchen with the brush, switched on the power, and began scrubbing her sneakers with vigor. It only made them worse. Pieces of white were flaking off her shoes and falling into the sink. Marta groaned. Why hadn't she thought ahead and put shoe polish in her duffle bag? Because she didn't think she'd need it, that's why. Her good shoes were still on a bus, probably in Canada by now. Not much point in searching the apartment for shoe polish. Ginger's taste in shoes seemed to run to leather sandals.

She glanced at the kitchen clock. Time was slipping by. Paint! She'd seen a gallon of paint by the kitchen door. *Oh, please, be white paint.* Marta grabbed a butter knife out of the drawer and knelt on the floor to pry off the lid. It wouldn't budge, but according to the label it was white paint, so she jiggled the knife harder. The blade bent and she had to give up. There must be a screwdriver around somewhere. Wouldn't Ginger's brother have one? It would be great if he'd show up and open this can of paint for her. Not! The whole point was to get away from him, not hope for his arrival.

The kitchen drawers didn't yield a screwdriver, but there was a bottle opener. Sure enough, the lid started to give as she used it to apply pressure around the top. The lid popped off so suddenly she had to jump to her feet to keep from getting hit in the face. White paint splattered on her hands, and a big glob landed on the floor. She could feel some of it between her toes. The paper towels were all the way across the kitchen and she'd leave footprints all the way over there if she went for them. There was no choice. This mess had to be cleaned up and before Josh got back.

Marta cautiously took a step on the slippery linoleum. The sound of a key turning in the front door lock reached her ears just as her feet slid out from under her.

CHAPTER TWO

Josh inspected the scene in front of him in disbelief. Every kitchen drawer was pulled out, and kitchen utensils littered the counter. A sneaker sat upside down in the sink next to his brand new electric toothbrush. Several feet of paper towels trailed across the floor from the sink, leading the way to the most fascinating picture of all. His houseguest knelt on the floor trying to scoop what appeared to be five gallons of paint, into a gallon can, using nothing but her bare hands.

"I'm sure you have a good explanation for all this."

Marta's dark brown eyes stood out starkly from a face nearly pale as the paint covering her arms and clothing. "I think the answer is obvious. I'm trying to clean up this mess." She attempted to stand, but seemed to have difficulty in getting enough traction. Just as she rose from her knees, a foot slid away from her body and her arms flailed in the air like a helicopter propeller.

"Don't move. You'll just track it all over."

"Don't worry. I'll clean up every last spot. If you could please hand me some towels, I'll get started."

Josh had to give her credit. She'd somehow managed to keep her composure in a situation that would have reduced his sister to tears. In fact his sister's tears were keeping him from throttling Marta right now. That very morning she had made him promise to let Marta stay with them till she got on her feet. Apparently Marta had always been there for Ginger when they were kids. The Lord knew he hadn't been. To cinch the deal, he had extracted a promise from Ginger to stop going unescorted to the downtown rescue missions. She'd halfheartedly made that same promise before and broken it. However, this time her friend's well-being was at stake. He planned to use that fact to his advantage.

He reached for a roll of paper towels, careful to avoid stepping in the wet paint. Where should he start? A garden hose seemed like the best solution. In fact, he would get a great deal of pleasure in turning a spray of cold water on this idiot female. Too bad this had to happen in his kitchen. Maybe he should just drag her outside.

"Are you going to just stand there grinning or are you going to hand me those towels?" Marta swiped at the towels with her hand, sending droplets of paint toward his legs.

"Hey! I said stay still." Josh stooped next to her and patted some paint off her arm. "I don't think one roll is going to do it. Here. You wipe the paint off yourself, and I'll go get some rags."

He stood, left the kitchen, and returned a few moments later with a bucket and a stack of old terry towels. While he filled the bucket with warm water, he watched her out of the corner of his eye. She was scrubbing at her hands and arms, but making little headway. The latex paint was already beginning to dry. How had she gotten herself into such a mess? Josh arranged his facial expression into a stern look. No need to let her think he was a softie. She'd probably only try and take advantage.

"Here. Let me do this for you." He set the bucket down and dipped the softest of the towels into the bucket. Starting with a spot on her chin, he gently cleaned the paint away. Her arms had reddened from her own efforts so he took his time cleansing her sensitive skin. This woman was definitely not a chatter box. The only sound he could hear was their combined breathing. Glancing from his task to her face, he was surprised to see she looked mortified.

"I guess you wanted to wear white to your job interview." He continued to move the moist towel over her hands and between her fingers. She didn't reply and he wondered if she'd lost her sense of humor. Come to think of it, he'd seen very little evidence of light heartedness in her since they'd met. Well, she'd better learn to laugh at herself if she was going to get along in this world.

Marta's face, arms, and hands were clean . . . or as clean as he could get them without the garden hose. Her silence, however, was aggravating. It wasn't every day he bathed a strange woman in his kitchen. She could at least talk to him. He grabbed her ankle and started washing her foot. She squawked and kicked at him, just barely missing.

"Stop screeching and hold still!"

"You're tickling me," she yelled and continued to kick. "Let go of my foot."

Josh firmly held her ankle and continued to dip and wash. He might as well be trying to bathe a cat, as much cooperation as she was giving him. Determined to see the job through, he seized her other ankle and stroked the wet cloth across her instep. He couldn't remember performing such an intimate task for a woman before. It certainly gave a whole new dimension to their association.

He glanced at her face and saw her eyes were closed. She had also stopped struggling. His hand holding her ankle relaxed and he used both hands to wash and massage her feet. Why hadn't he ever noticed how pretty a woman's foot was before? The way the arch curved and the delicate bone structure claimed his attention.

"You're not one of those foot fetishists are you?" Her soft question broke his concentration.

"A what?"

"You know . . . a person who fixates on weird objects like feet?"

Josh pulled his hands away, causing her feet to land with a thunk on the wet floor. "I assure you, lady, I'm not *fixated* on any part of you. I'm merely trying to clean up this mess you've made before you ruin my entire apartment. Which brings me back to my original question; what's going on here?"

It's a long story." She sighed.

Josh stood and pulled her to her feet. "I've got time to listen while we clean up this kitchen." He couldn't wait to hear her explanation. It was bound to be a doozy. "Well?"

"I wanted to look presentable when I hunted for a job. I was trying to get my sneakers white and things got a little

15

out of hand. Now I'll never find work. I can't go anywhere dressed like this." She rubbed at a stain on her jeans.

"Well, you could always look for a job as a painter. Your wardrobe would fit right in."

"I don't find that a bit funny."

"I didn't mean it to be funny." He watched her mouth set into a grim line. "O.K., I guess I did. It's just that . . ." he chuckled, "oh, never mind."

"Never mind? You're the one who was so hot to see me leave. Frankly I can't wait to get away from this place. However, I can't very well leave without a job."

"So, you're serious about finding work?"

"Of course, I'm serious. Did you think I was going to sponge off Ginger the rest of my life?"

Josh flushed guiltily. That was very close to what he'd been thinking. He knew he was going to regret it, but something about her compelled him to help. "You can come to work for me." The minute the words were out of his mouth, he wanted to call them back. On the other hand, what better opportunity to find out what she was really up to?

"Thanks anyway, but I don't think so. I'll find something on my own."

Josh wondered what kind of job she thought she would find. Here he was, offering her a helping hand, and she was rejecting it. A typical woman. All fired up to prove her independence. She'd soon find out how hard it was going to be for her and come begging him for help. Or . . . maybe she really didn't want to work at all.

"If you're afraid of a little hard work, you probably wouldn't fit in with the rest of my crew, anyway. For now, why don't you concentrate on putting my kitchen back in order?" He dropped the dirty rags in the bucket and turned to the door. "And from now on, keep your hands off my things. When I get back from work, I'll expect to find you've bought me a new toothbrush to replace the one you destroyed."

16

***

Marta exhaled in relief as the door closed behind Josh's back. She'd felt like a mouse in a trap with him there. His presence had positively filled the tiny kitchen and made her crave escape. She emptied the bucket and refilled it with warm water. It was going to take all morning to clean up the mess she'd made, but there was no one to blame but herself. She didn't appreciate Josh's attitude, however. He'd laughed at her. She hated that. Didn't the man have a shred of sympathy? Did he think she'd deliberately set out to trash the kitchen?

She felt her cheeks grow hot at the remembrance of his hands washing her bare feet. No man had ever touched her that way. Or made her want to give in to the pampered feeling. She didn't like the thought of anyone having that kind of power over her.

Marta spent the next hour wiping away every speck of paint from the floor. Then she decided she might as well continue cleaning the kitchen since she was already dirty and sweaty. There wasn't much chance of getting her act together to hunt for a job till the next day. Now she needed to readjust her goal.

No. The goal was still the same; get a new life . . . a good life. It was just going to take a little longer than she'd planned. She scrubbed the stove top and oven. From the looks of the remnants of tomato sauce and cheese, Ginger, and probably Josh, too, had been living on pizza and other assorted takeout food. Marta resolved to cook them at least one decent meal before she moved out. It would be a celebration meal.

She collapsed on a kitchen chair, physically and emotionally exhausted. The newspaper caught her eye and she ran her finger down the help wanted columns again, stopping when she noticed her red and swollen index finger. In fact, both her hands were red and itchy. The print blurred as she read. *It must be the fumes from the paint and the stuff I cleaned the oven with.* Fresh air. That's what she needed. Taking

17

the paper with her, she rose and opened a window. The cold breeze felt good and the smell from the recent rain helped chase the chemical stench away.

One of the ads asked for a receptionist. Pleasant phone voice was a *must*. Applicants were instructed to call for an appointment. Well, that shouldn't be too hard. She'd call right now and worry about clothes for the interview later. Even with all the fresh air blowing into the room, her eyes were burning. She could barely make out the phone number, but found if she squinted, she could make it out. She moved over to the phone and punched the numbers.

"Good afternoon. Brinkly Associates. How may I help you?"

"Hello. My name is Marta Petrosky. I'm calling to inquire about the receptionist position you advertised."

"Yes, MS Petrosky. We're setting up interviews this week. The position is in the front office and the person filling it is required to greet walk-in traffic and handle all the phones."

Marta's heart fell. The job was going to require a nice wardrobe. She couldn't borrow anything from Ginger. Even if they were the same size, which they weren't, Ginger's clothes were hardly appropriate for an office. However, if she could postpone the interview for a few days, she might have time to find a few things in a consignment shop.

"That sounds like just the job I'm looking for. When would it be convenient for me to come in and fill out an application?"

"We need someone right away. It's my job we're filling and I'm leaving on maternity leave the end of the week. Might I say, you have a very pleasing voice? If you make the same impression in person, I'm sure you'll have a good chance of getting hired. Could you come in tomorrow?"

Tomorrow? How could she ever be ready for an interview in time? It didn't matter how hard it was going to be. Only one nice outfit would be needed by tomorrow. She'd manage somehow. She *needed* a job.

"Yes, tomorrow's fine. Would an afternoon appointment be available?"

"Certainly MS Petrosky. I have you down for one o'clock."

Marta hung up the phone after getting directions to the office. Her eyes were still burning, but it was getting icy cold in the room so she closed the window. Maybe if she splashed some water on her face. Her jeans were dry by now, so she would put on some lipstick and walk to the store. She hadn't forgotten about replacing Josh's toothbrush. She retrieved it from the sink to take with her so she'd be sure and replace it with the identical brand. It would be a good idea to get some hand lotion, too. Or find something that would relieve the itching. She'd never had an allergic reaction to anything before . . . with the exception of cats. Ginger should have remembered that when she had told Josh she wanted to get a cat. Fat chance. The minute a cat came within a block of her, the sneezing and coughing started.

Marta tried to recall how far it was to the store. She remembered passing one the night before, but it had been dark and Ginger was driving. At least she knew the general direction. Pulling the cap off her lipstick, she turned to face the mirror.

"Oh dear!" The gruesome sight in the mirror couldn't be her. It just couldn't. A red swollen face with two little slits for eyes? It must be some allergic reaction. What was she going to do now? She couldn't possibly go outside looking like this. People would run away screaming. Marta moaned. Her breath caught. What if she was going into anaphylactic shock? She would die in a strange city with only Ginger and maybe, her scornful brother, attending her funeral. She would never realize her dreams, have her own elegant home, or have witty successful friends. Her life hadn't even begun yet. She had to get help. Now.

Slowly she worked her way down the hallway, leaning on the wall for support. Everything was a big blur. Marta

19

tried to focus on the table where the telephone was. Who would she call? She didn't know Ginger's number at work. 911? Out of the question. She had no money for doctors or hospitals. Since she was still a legal resident of Oregon, she probably wouldn't qualify for medical assistance in Seattle.

She finally made it to the front door and outside. She felt a rush of relief she hadn't knocked anything over and broken it on the way. It would have been just one more reason for Josh to boot her out on the street. "Help! Could someone please help me?" It was a struggle to get the words out. Nobody answered. Was everyone at work?

"Help!" Marta slumped to the ground. She gripped the porch rail with one hand, grateful for anything solid to cling to.

***

Josh was just putting the finishing touches of stain on an apartment door nearby when he heard someone shout "FIRE!" His heart stopped in sheer terror. He dropped his brush and ran toward the cry. Not a fire! Not here in his apartment building. There were families living here. Little kids, probably taking naps right now in their cribs. His and Ginger's future were tied up in these buildings. He was gasping for breath by the time he rounded the corner of the building and spied Marta hunched over on the steps.

"Where's the fire? Did you call the fire department yet?" He should have known. Only this lame brain woman would have started a fire in his building. "Answer me!" He raced up the steps past Marta and entered the apartment, searching for a sign of smoke and finding none. The kitchen was fresh smelling and immaculate. His frantic search through the bedrooms didn't uncover any sign of a fire either. He ran back outside. Marta sat on the bottom step, her head in her hands.

"Are you the one who yelled 'fire' or not?" He wanted to shake her . . . anything to get a response. What kind of game was she playing? His heart had started back up with vigor, pounding in his chest and filling his ears with its heavy drumbeat. It nearly drowned out her response.

"Yes. No."

Josh grasped Marta's wrist and pulled it away from her face. "Did you yell, 'fire', or not?"

"Yes." She wouldn't look at him, and her hair was hiding her face. He wanted to see her face . . . to confirm she thought this was some funny joke.

"Why did you yell, 'fire'? I don't smell any smoke. I don't see a fire. All I see is YOU sitting here with your shoulders shaking with laughter. I could wring your pretty neck."

"I hollered for help. Nobody came. I'd heard if a person yelled out, 'fire', help would come."

"Of all the stupid- This is the last straw." Josh, still holding her wrist, yanked her to her feet. He was mad, but worse than that, he'd been scared. He whirled her around to face him. He was really going to give her a dressing down. Never mind his promise to Ginger. Marta was going to go.

The full force of her weight pulled his arm as he tried to hold her upright. Then he saw her face. It resembled a red grapefruit that had been left out in the sun too long. It was probably the most gruesome sight he'd ever seen, and he suddenly felt ashamed.

"Marta? Honey? What happened to you?"

Her face distorted into a huge grimace as her mouth opened to speak, but no words came out.

Josh knew about symptoms like this and had been severely warned about the consequences. That was why he carried an epi-pen with him. He was deathly allergic to bee stings.

"We've got to get you to a doctor."

"No. I don't want a doctor." Her speech was muffled, but if he held his ear close, he could understand her.

The frantic waving of her hands dispelled any notion she would allow him to take her to the emergency room. He had to do something. She looked like she was in pain. He scooped her up in his arms, carried her into the apartment and gently laid her on the couch. He trotted to the bathroom and pulled open the medicine chest. He didn't want to give epinephrine unless absolutely necessary. He'd start with an antihistamine and see if that would give her any relief. He grabbed the bottle and brought it and a cold glass of water back to the living room.

Marta hadn't moved from the spot where he'd laid her. She looked even more miserable than before. He sat next to her and tenderly cradling her head in his left arm, he put a pill in her mouth and held the glass to her lips. He'd never seen such swollen lips. He tried to be gentle and was relieved when she swallowed the pill and water. He gave her another sip of water, hoping the cool liquid would be soothing. It seemed to help, yet he continued to hold her against him, listening for any sign of labored breathing.

Josh recalled holding his younger sisters just this way when they had the measles. He couldn't have been much older than twelve then. It made him feel strong and protective when they had clung to him because their parents were no longer around. Ginger, especially, had looked up to him and followed him around. Irene was another story. She always wanted things her own way and didn't listen to him much. He'd ultimately let them both down. He'd vowed to do whatever it took to make it up to them.

"Oh Father, I don't know why you sent her here, but I know you must have a plan. Please comfort and protect her now and if it is Your will, heal her body. In Jesus's precious name, amen."

Marta stirred in his arms. Her breathing was less raspy now, and she appeared to be sleeping. The pill he'd given her was known to cause drowsiness, so he wasn't surprised. He searched her face to determine if the swelling was going down. It was still puffy. Her swollen features differed significantly from the lovely face he'd first seen the night before. He shook his head in bafflement. Had it really been less than twenty-four hours since she'd arrived?

Josh looked at his watch and realized he'd been sitting with her for over an hour. Not much point in working anymore today. She shouldn't be left alone and he wouldn't be able to concentrate on his job while worrying about her. He rose from the couch and covered her with an afghan. It would only take a few minutes to gather his tools and supplies and put them away. Then he'd return and wait for her to wake up. He planned to have a talk with her about home safety and the hazards of mixing chemicals.

***

"Marta. Marta, are you awake?" Ginger's voice reached Marta through the sleepy fog of her consciousness. "Marta?"

"I'm awake . . . barely. You're home. What time is it?"

"It's nearly six o'clock. Josh says you've been sleeping for hours. He had to run some errands, but he left orders for me to feed you some soup. Are you feeling any better?"

"Orders? Josh gave you orders?" Just the word *orders* jerked her to full alert.

"I don't mind. Josh is usually right, anyway. Would you like crackers with your soup?"

Marta's stomach growled at the thought of food. She realized she hadn't eaten anything since breakfast. "I'd love some crackers, but you don't have to wait on me. I'm well enough to get up." She swung her legs to the floor and gingerly stood, swaying only slightly. Whatever Josh had given her must have been strong. The room had a crazy tilt to it.

As Ginger averted her eyes and turned toward the kitchen, Marta noticed something different. "Ginger, wasn't your hair maroon this morning?"

"I added a new color. Do you like it?" She patted her frizzy blond curls which had replaced the maroon spikes. "I thought about what you said. You know. Making something of yourself? And I thought I'd go with something a little more conservative."

"Uh, it's very nice, Ginger. It's you. Fits your personality." Marta really didn't want to dwell on

23

appearances and success right now. If what she'd seen in the mirror that morning was linked to her future, the outlook was very bleak indeed.

"Thanks. Don't forget. I promised to do a makeover on you anytime you want."

A rush of gratitude toward her friend for not adding how awful she looked warmed Marta's heart. "Thanks, Ginger. I think I'll stay away from chemicals for a while, though." Far away. Marta's face still felt tight. Her hands and arms had quit itching, though. She sat and took a sip of the soup. Then she remembered her job interview. Could she make herself presentable by tomorrow? She'd have to race the clock in the morning if she was going to find clothes, find the right bus route, and still make it in time.

"Ginger, is there a clothing consignment shop near here?"

"There's one in that strip mall about two miles past the grocery store. Why?"

"I need some nice clothes. I've got a job interview tomorrow."

Ginger pulled up a chair across from Marta and passed her the crackers. "Marta, I don't know if you should go out tomorrow. You've had quite a traumatic experience today. And . . . your face is still pretty puffy."

"You don't have to remind me about my face. It still feels funny. I'm sure I'll be back to normal by tomorrow, though. I have to get to that interview. I already have an appointment and the woman on the phone sounded encouraging."

"I don't know, Marta. I don't think it's a good idea for you to go out so soon. Why don't you wait and see what Josh says?"

"This has nothing to do with Josh. I don't need your brother's permission to leave the apartment. Honestly, Ginger. You really are too dependent on him."

24

"Oh, Marta. I was hoping you'd like my brother. I even secretly hoped you two might hit it off and get together. Don't you think he's just way too handsome?"

This was worse than Marta thought. Not only was Ginger blind when it came to her brother, she was going to try and play matchmaker, too. "I suppose he's attractive . . . in a rugged sort of way. But there are lots of attractive men in the world, Ginger. That doesn't mean I have anything in common with them."

Disapproval showed in Ginger's face. "You mean, because he's not rich?"

"There's nothing wrong with marrying a man who can provide security," Marta replied defensively. *A man who wasn't bossy and controlling like Josh.* She kept that thought to herself. "I hope you haven't encouraged your brother to ask me out or anything like that. I don't have time to get sidetracked on a relationship that is doomed to fail."

"If you'd just give Josh a chance-"

"No. Ginger, please. You've been my very best friend and always will be. But there's no future for your brother and me. We don't even like each other very much. Please respect my decision to plan my own life." Marta reached out and took Ginger's hand to help soften her words.

Ginger's eyes predictably filled with tears. "You'd better eat your soup before it gets cold," she said.

Marta finished her soup and headed for the bathroom to wash up and check out her face. To her dismay, it looked nearly as bad as it had earlier. How long was she going to look like a monster? She dreaded the thought this might be a permanent condition. The only job she was fit for in her present state was a receptionist at a haunted house . . . seasonal work to be sure. Besides, Halloween was a month off. Her money would run out before then.

As she made her way back to the kitchen, she heard Josh and Ginger talking. So he'd returned. She would be pleasant to him for her friend's sake. But that was all. Cool, polite and distant, but *pleasant.*

25

"Hello, Josh. I haven't thanked you for coming to my rescue this morning."

He turned and smiled at her, not hiding the fact he was inspecting her inflated lips, cheeks and eyes. His demeanor suggested he was humoring a sick child. "No need to thank me. I'm glad to see you up and about. Now what's this about a job interview tomorrow?"

"I'm expected at Brinkly & Associates tomorrow at one. However, I'll be leaving early in the morning to run some errands first. I have to get started on a suitable wardrobe."

"No need to do that. I've taken care of it for you."

"You what?"

"When I was out getting a new toothbrush that you neglected to replace for me, I picked up a few things for you to wear on your new job. Here." He thrust a plastic bag, imprinted with the name of a discount store, at her.

Marta clenched her fists. "I didn't ask you to shop for me and you know very well why I didn't buy you a new toothbrush today. I can't imagine what kind of appropriate clothing you could find for me. You don't even know my size." She pushed the bag back toward him.

"The size part was easy. I bought you some one-size-fits-all things." He removed a stack of coveralls from the bag. "I even got you a pair in each color."

Marta stared at the pile of hideous work clothes then up at Josh and decided then and there she genuinely disliked him. "Are you nuts? I wouldn't be caught dead in those. Those are for men. Mechanics. Plumbers or laborers."

"That's what you're going to do. Labor."

"I am not. I'm going to work in a nice office."

"Who's going to hire you? Have you looked in a mirror?"

"You're mean, you know that? Of course I've looked in a mirror. I'll be fine by tomorrow."

"And then what? You'll find a job paying little better than a minimum wage? You'll have to spend your first few

26

paychecks buying clothes. And don't forget your bus fare back and forth to work."

"I thought you wanted me to find a job."

"I told you. You can work for me."

"No way,"

Ginger spoke up, "Oh please, Marta. If you're working close by, we can spend more time together. If you took that other job, you'd probably have to transfer buses at least three times. I'll bet the commute would be at least an hour each way."

"Well at least I'd be working in a good part of the city." Why did it feel like Josh and Ginger were ganging up on her? She knew Ginger's motives, but what did Josh have to gain? Maybe she should take his old job, just to aggravate him. He'd soon be begging her to find something else.

"I suppose it would give me a chance to build a savings account." It would also give her an opportunity to convince Ginger that a romance between her and Josh would never work. And who knows? Once she got a real job and could afford to get her own place, she might be able to persuade Ginger to move with her . . . away from her domineering brother.

She glanced from Josh to Ginger who were both looking at her expectantly.

"I guess it wouldn't hurt to try it, but just temporarily." She couldn't wait to get started. She'd wipe that smug look off Josh's face when she was living in Seattle's equivalent of Beverly Hills.

CHAPTER THREE

Josh busied himself in the tool shed while waiting for Marta to show for her first day of work. He had some doubts she'd appear after the fit she'd thrown that morning. Why she got so mad about him calling and canceling her interview, he couldn't understand. He was only trying to help. Tying up a loose end seemed the right thing to do. Instead of being grateful for his help, she had lambasted him for butting in.

After that, it hadn't seemed like the right time to warn her against taking another antihistamine tablet. Now she'd probably fall asleep on the job. He'd have to make sure he didn't give her anything dangerous to do. He felt more like a babysitter than an employer. Well, it couldn't be helped. Ginny would never forgive him if Marta got hurt on the job.

Marta suddenly appeared in the doorway, her silhouette backlit by the morning sunlight. Tiny wisps of hair had escaped the thick brown curls tied behind her neck. She was wearing bright blue coveralls, cinched in tightly at the waist. Josh sucked in his breath at the way the sun backlit her hair like a halo. If she weren't so contrary, he might even enjoy this babysitting job.

Josh swallowed and cleared his throat. "Are you ready to get started?"

"Yes, but we need to get a few things straight first." She stood with her feet planted slightly apart and her hands on her hips.

"Such as?"

"I will work for you. But, I must be very clear . . . it's only temporary."

"I understand. *Now* are you ready to start?"

"Not quite yet." She jutted her chin. "I will put in a day's work for a day's pay. However, I expect to get paid the same wage as any other member of the crew doing the same job. Where is the rest of your crew, anyway?"

"You're it, kiddo. It's just you and me." He resisted the sudden urge to reach out and tweak her nose. "Anything else?"

"Just one more thing. I'd like some flexibility in my work schedule so I can go on job interviews. I would still put in all the hours I'm paid for, you understand."

"I wouldn't have it any other way. Now can we please get started?"

"Just tell me what you'd like me to do first."

What he'd like her to do involved her lips, which were slightly pouty looking from yesterday's incident. Maybe they'd better move outside. It was getting pretty warm in the shed, with the two of them of them standing so close. He motioned her outside and picked up the piece of equipment he intended for her to use.

"This is a backpack blower. It's used for cleaning the leaves and dirt off the sidewalks and parking lot. You put your arms through these straps, turn on the little switch and I'll pull the starter rope for you."

"I can do it myself, thank you." Marta took the blower from him and after a few clumsy attempts, finally got it settled firmly on her back. She easily found the switch near her waist, but when she tried pulling the starter rope, she didn't have enough leverage. "I guess I'm still a little weak. Could you start it for me?"

"I'll do it for you this time so you can see how it's done. If you turn it off and can't find me, just start it *before* you hoist it to your shoulders. You're going to run out of gasoline in about an hour. There's a can of mixed gas in the shed. If the noise bothers you, there're earplugs in the shed too."

"OK, OK, just start the thing and let me get to work." Marta hoped he wasn't going to hang over her shoulder all morning. Did he think she was helpless? She braced her feet, but still nearly fell when he yanked the starter rope. He was probably laughing at her but she refused to look at him and marched off to the nearest parking lot to tackle the leaves.

From the appearance of the lot, it hadn't been cleaned since the first fall rain. Red and gold leaves of every description had piled up to a foot deep in places. How the tenants found their assigned parking spaces was a mystery to her. Apart from the deafening noise of the blower, Marta rather enjoyed her task. The October sun was climbing higher in the sky adding even more vividness to the colors on the ground and trees. Not exactly the job she'd envisioned, but a nice interlude just the same.

Soon she had huge piles of pretty leaves stacked at either end of the parking lot. She switched off the blower and removed it from her back. It would have been tempting to dive into the middle of one of the piles, surrounding herself with the brilliant fall colors, but she was determined to show Josh she wasn't the incompetent fool he thought. She caught glimpses of him watching her as she removed the piles, filling the dumpster, but deliberately ignored him.

Not bad for only an hour's work. She was pleased with herself. Hoisting the blower to her shoulder, she walked to an adjacent parking lot. This one was going to be more difficult. There were several cars parked there and a lot of trash littered the area. Setting the blower on the ground, she flipped on the switch and gave the starter rope a hard tug. Nothing happened. She yanked harder, and the motor still refused to catch. She was already breathing hard and could feel beads of sweat pop up on her forehead. It must have been that antihistamine she'd taken that morning. She usually had a lot more energy.

"Did you refill the gas tank?"

Marta glared at Josh. Had he been hiding in the bushes just waiting to pounce out and catch her in a mistake? "I was just going to do that."

"Would you like me to show you how?"

"No!" Marta was really getting annoyed at his perpetual role of superior male. Did he think she was a child? She hefted the blower and stalked back to the tool shed, positive the thing must have weighed at least fifty pounds. It should have felt lighter, considering the gas tank was apparently empty.

Marta congratulated herself on stumbling only once. There was no way she was going to let on how groggy she felt. And why was he following her to the tool shed? Didn't he have work of his own to do? She found the gas can and filled the leaf blower with no problem. She didn't even spill any gasoline or start any fires. That should comfort Mr. High and Mighty. She turned to leave the shed, observing Josh opening his mouth, evidently to give her further instructions. Just for good measure, she patted the ear plugs she'd put in. Instead of taking a hint, his mouth continued to move.

"Sorry. I can't hear you." She easily started the blower, relieved when it started at her first try and walked away leaving Josh standing with his mouth moving like a goldfish's. The second parking lot went a lot faster. She was getting the hang of it. The earplugs blocked out everything but her own thoughts . . . thoughts of her future, which definitely didn't include wearing grubby men's clothing and working for Josh.

***

Marta stepped out of the silver stretch limo. Her date for the evening took her hand, briefly touching his lips to her upturned palm. She brushed the folds of her shimmering satin gown, pleased with the way it draped to the ground, just barely skimming the top of her five-hundred dollar Italian pumps. She didn't need to look around to know how many admiring glances, from both men and women, were sent her way. She had done this many times before. Marta extended her arm, generously waving to the crowd who was also waiting to enter the Opera House.

***

"Hey! Watch it! You're blowing dust all over my wet paint!"

Marta's eyes flew open and saw she had indeed blown dirt and leaves right toward Josh, who was glowering at her. As usual. He looked like he'd like to wrap his paintbrush

31

around her neck. "It was an accident." Couldn't he cut her any slack at all? And did he have to yell? She could hear him quite plainly, even with her earplugs in.

"I've been trying to get your attention for the last ten minutes, but you act like you're in a trance or something. Did you take some more of those allergy pills?"

"No, I was only daydreaming. I'm sorry. How many times do I have to apologize?" Blockhead. She wasn't exactly thrilled to be jolted back to reality by a painter in a blue flannel shirt. Now if he'd been wearing a tux- "I'll go around to the other side of the building."

"Waht ow fo caws." Josh's voice sounded muffled. He must have quit yelling.

"I can't hear you with these earplugs in. Goodbye." She left him to his mumbling whatever it was he was mumbling and headed for the opposite side of the apartment complex, stopping along the way to refill the gas tank.

The entire apartment complex was made up of four separate buildings. Each building contained eight apartments; four on the ground and four on the second story. The building Ginger and Josh lived in was fully rented, as was the building right next to it. Josh was apparently putting the finishing touches on the third building. Marta stood in front of the last building and noted its shabby rundown appearance. If all the buildings had once looked like this, Josh had already put a tremendous amount of work into the complex.

Even though it appeared no one would be using the area for quite some time, Marta figured she might as well remove the leaves and debris before the wind blew it all over. She didn't mind the work, but wished she could conjure up a face to go with the man in the tuxedo in her daydream. He'd have to be at least as good looking as Josh. Older, probably. And kind. She'd never been able to imagine exactly what her future husband might look like. She knew she'd recognize him when she met him, though.

Several times she had to stop and pick up broken glass from the parking lot. Later she would return with a broom and dustpan to get the small fragments. Leaves and garbage had blown into the apartment entryways. A rain gutter had broken loose from the porch roof and one end hung down, allowing Marta to see it was clogged with leaves and pine needles. If she could somehow use the blower to clean it out, it might prevent the whole thing from crashing down. Every gutter on the building was probably in the same shape.

Since she had to find a broom, she might as well look for a ladder at the same time. She found both items in the tool shed. She might have known. Josh had his faults, but he seemed to be compulsively organized. In fact, she was surprised he didn't have his tools lined up in alphabetical order. Instead, he had them hanging on a pegboard, arranged according to size. Marta lifted the step ladder from its hooks on the wall, and carried it and the broom back to the vacant building.

Climbing the ladder with the blower on her back was awkward, to say the least. The ground was soft from the recent rains and Marta prayed the thing wouldn't tip over with her on it. She climbed to the fourth step and was able to blow most of the debris from the hanging gutter, but couldn't reach the ones still attached to the building. What she needed was an extension ladder, but she hadn't seen one in the shed. She had seen one leaning against one of the other buildings, however.

Marta set out to get the longer ladder, proud of herself for showing so much initiative. Just let Josh find something to complain about now. Maybe he was already noticing what a good worker she was, he hadn't been around to check on her for quite a while. The silver extension ladder was leaning against the building right where she remembered seeing it. Her employer was nowhere in sight. If she hurried, she could borrow the ladder and have it back in its place by lunchtime.

She grasped the ladder with both hands and tried to lift it away from the building. The thing was heavier than it looked. Wasn't aluminum supposed to be lighter in weight than wood? Somehow, she was going to have to slide it gently to the ground and fold it into a more manageable size if she was going to carry it to the other building. If she pushed it a little to the left, she could tip it into that big holly tree. After that, she could reach up and unhook the doodads that locked it into its extended state, making it much easier to carry.

Little by little, she slid the ladder along the building and toward the tree. The building had a fresh coat of paint on it, so she took her time. When she judged she was close enough to pitch the ladder toward the tree, she pulled the ladder away from the wall.

"Get your hands off that ladder!"

Marta jumped, and in the process, the aluminum monster took on a life of its own and swung away from the building. "Oh, no!" She pushed it back as hard as she could but misjudged her strength. It slammed back into the building, tipped at an angle and firmly lodged itself through a plate glass window. The crash of breaking glass drowned out most of Josh's words, but she could tell he was probably mad. Where was he, anyway? She looked behind her and couldn't see him anywhere.

"You crazy woman! Are you deliberately trying to destroy my apartment building?"

Marta squinted into the sun. His voice had come from somewhere above her. "Oh, there you are. I was wondering where you were." Josh was kneeling on the roof and his body language suggested he wasn't happy to see her. She backed up a few steps, shading her eyes with her hands.

"Oh no, you don't. You're not going to take off and leave me here."

"I was only trying to get a better look. And you don't have to bellow at me. I took the earplugs out."

"Bellow? BELLOW? You haven't heard anything yet. Now put that ladder back where I had it so I can come down there and really tell you what I think."

"I think its kinda stuck. Could you climb down that tree or something?"

"That's not a tree! It's a blooming sticker bush!"

"It's not really bloom-"

"Marta!"

"OK, I'll try to move the ladder, but I didn't have very good luck the first time."

***

"Just do it." It took every bit of Josh's self-control to wait quietly while Marta struggled with the ladder. His jaw ached from clenching his teeth together. He could almost taste the angry words stuck in his throat, but instinctively knew if he said anything else, that flighty air head below would walk off and leave him sitting on the roof. Whatever possessed him to turn his back on her? The woman was downright dangerous. He began praying for patience.

Her strained voice drifted up toward him. "I think I've just about got it."

Marta had one foot braced on the freshly painted siding and was tugging on the ladder. Josh heard a fresh shower of glass fall with each tug. At this rate, this was going to take all day. He thought about having her go up the stairs to the second story apartment and push the ladder from inside the broken window, but discarded the idea. With his luck, and hers, she'd probably cut herself and bleed to death before anyone found them.

"Maybe I should go for help."

"Try it one more time, Marta."

"I've *been* trying, or hadn't you noticed? I was thinking if we could get a fire truck here . . . one with a ladder, they could get you off the roof in no time at all."

"The fire department doesn't respond to non-life-threatening situations, Marta."

35

"I don't know why not. They rescue cats up in trees. I saw it on television."

Josh flirted with the idea of jumping from the roof. If he aimed his descent just right, Marta's body might provide a really soft landing. His feet itched to pace back and forth as he waited to be rescued, but the steep pitch of the roof didn't allow even that small comfort.

"That's only on television . . . not in real life. Try lifting the ladder and pulling the bottom away from the building." He sat and waited for the sounds of more windows breaking, but it was eerily silent. "Marta?" He peered over the edge. She was gone!

Josh slammed his fist on the roof so hard it broke the skin on his knuckles. How could she go off and leave him there? He should have known if he prayed for patience, he'd get adversity. After all he'd done to try and help her, this is how she thanked him? What was he supposed to do . . . wait till dark when his tenants started arriving home from work? He looked at his watch. It was nearly one o'clock. Perhaps his dingbat helper had just gone for a bite of lunch. She would probably be back soon, smacking her lips from eating the roast beef sandwich he had made for himself that morning.

Was it only two days ago she'd arrived? He'd suspected from the start, she would be nothing but trouble. Little had he known how much trouble she would be, or he would have personally put her on a bus back to Portland the minute she arrived on his doorstep. But, noooo. He'd let his sister talk him into letting her stay. To be honest, something about Marta, herself, had swayed him, too. Probably the clever persona she had invented to get her own way. Dumb him. It had apparently worked. He'd let those beautiful brown eyes and an even more beautiful mouth temporarily get to him.

The sound of voices reached him, and to his relief, they were getting closer. Marta came into view and was speaking animatedly to the mail carrier. The white haired guy was

36

pushing a handcart full of mail. He'd given up carrying a mail bag years before when old age began to slow him down. He'd once told Josh retirement wasn't an option for him. He'd miss the folks on his route too much and was lonely since his wife had passed away. Judging by his reaction to the way Marta was batting her eyes at him, his advanced age didn't prevent him from enjoying a pretty woman. He hadn't even once glanced up to where Josh was impatiently waiting.

Josh didn't hold out much hope for the mailman's ability to rescue him. He barely had the strength to heft more than a few pieces of junk mail at a time into the upper mail slots. The fire department was beginning to look more and more like a desirable option. At least they wouldn't get injured and sue him.

"I don't think you'd better try moving that ladder, Mr. Whitestone," Josh called.

The old man peered up at him. "Oh, I wasn't going to. I was just chatting with Marta, here. You got yourself into some predicament, doncha? I remember one time something similar happened to me. Musta been right after World War two. Or was it the Korean War? I'd locked myself right out of my house. Had to break a window to get in. Guess that wouldn't help in your case, though. Your window's already broken."

No kidding, Josh thought. Just the kind of intelligent thinking that was needed in this situation. It was obvious he couldn't depend on anyone for help. He was going to have to take matters in his own hands. Then he was going to take a certain lily white neck in his hands and-

"There you are, you old coot!" Miss Treymore, spinster librarian, and his first tenant, came shuffling around the building, swinging her ivory handled cane over her head like a lasso. "How can I watch my programs when you can't even deliver my TV Guide on time? I should have known I'd find you dallying around, shirking your sworn oath to deliver the mail." She advanced on Marta and the mail man, jabbing the air with her cane, causing the wrinkled folds of skin on her upper arms to quiver and shake like the fall leaves.

"Now, now, Miss Treymore," Mr. Whitestone chided, "your programs are on at the same time every day. You don't need any TV Guide. You're just jealous because I'm out here talking to a beautiful young woman."

"Beautiful? Dressed like that? Look at her. She wouldn't know fashion if it jumped out of a catalog and bit her. That's the trouble with the younger generation. They have no respect or appreciation for the finer things in life."

"I do appreciate nice things," Marta protested. "Really. I have nicer clothes. It's just that Josh insisted I wear this."

"Josh? Are you speaking of that nice boy who's my landlord?"

"Of course that's who she's talkin' about. And that's why I'm staying right here to make sure he doesn't do anything else to harm her. She needs protection, her being a homeless orphan and all."

"Oh, you poor little thing," Miss Treymore crooned to Marta. "Why don't you come up to my apartment and I'll fix you a nice cup of chamomile tea?" Josh had heard enough. He had to get down off the roof before the crowd of lunatics below multiplied. He inched over to the edge of the roof as close as he could get to the holly tree. He closed his eyes briefly to offer up another prayer. The two old folks below were still fussing over poor Marta when he jumped.

CHAPTER FOUR

Marta read the list Josh had hastily scribbled and shook her head in disbelief. "According to this, if I work eight hours per day the rest of this week, by Friday I'll owe you eighty-four dollars and thirteen cents."

Josh looked up from dabbing iodine on the long scratches along his arms. "Is there a problem? I itemized everything for you."

"I can understand about the toothbrush and was going to replace it anyway. And I suppose I could reimburse you for the work clothes, even though I won't have much use for anything this ugly after I leave here. But you want me to pay for the entire window? After all, it was an accident. Don't you have insurance that covers accidents?"

"Yup. But the deductible is so high, the insurance won't cover replacing the window. As it is, I think I'm being pretty generous by not charging you for installation. I'll do that myself."

Marta knit her eyebrows together. "And what's this? You're charging me for a shirt? You didn't buy me a shirt."

"Nope. You're buying *me* a shirt . . . to replace the one that was ruined when I had to get off the roof via the holly tree."

"Well nobody asked you to go crashing through that tree like that. You nearly scared Miss Treymore half to death."

"Not half as badly as she scared me when she tried to give me mouth to mouth resuscitation."

Marta couldn't help but grin, remembering how Miss Treymore had immediately shuffled over to the base of the holly tree and checked Josh out for injuries. The elderly woman had first felt his arms and legs, checking for broken bones. It was only after Josh failed to answer and having problems catching his breath that she pinched his nose and started breathing for him. He came to almost right away and judging from the way he'd thrashed around, his injuries weren't too serious.

"Miss Treymore says she had a legal and moral obligation to administer first aid since her certification was up to date."

"Well, there ought to be a law against pounding on someone's chest with a cane, without first checking to see if a heartbeat is really absent."

Marta couldn't help herself. Her grin turned to laughter. She looked at Josh who wasn't laughing or even smiling. The corners of his mouth were twitching, though. Their eyes locked and Marta was about to point out the humor he had missed in the situation when the back door burst open and Ginger sailed in.

"Hi you two! It looks like you're getting along great. I just knew you would. Did you have a good day?" She planted a kiss on Josh's forehead and looked expectantly at Marta.

"Uh, well I cleaned all the parking lots and sidewalks."

"And just look how rosy your cheeks are from being out in all that fresh air. Most of my customers would just die to have a complexion like yours. Josh, you're such a dear brother for taking care of Marta like this. She's always been more of a sister to me than our own sister, and I've always wanted to pay her back for all the nice things she's done for me. Thanks to you, we're together again and life is just great."

"Ginger, you know I love you like a sister, too," Marta replied. "It isn't necessary for you to do anything to earn that love." Marta meant every word she said. Life had not been easy for either woman when they were growing up, but for Ginger, it been especially hard. Ginger *needed* family around her, whereas Marta had resigned herself to being an orphan. That didn't stop her from dreaming of having a storybook husband and her own home, though. That's all she needed.

40

"Josh, aren't we super lucky that Marta has come to live with us? It's an answer to prayer. I've got my best friend here now, and you've got a full time helper."

Josh mumbled something unintelligible and continued swabbing iodine on his cuts and scratches. He stood and took off his torn shirt, revealing several deep scratches on his back.

"Josh! What happened to your back?" Ginny exclaimed.

"Nothing a new helper wouldn't cure."

"The Lord sent you a new helper . . . a great one. Isn't that what I've been saying since I got home? Those are some pretty nasty scrapes. I've got some herbal salve that would be just the thing for that. Marta can put it on those scratches while I take a quick shower and start dinner." Ginny rummaged around in the cupboard and pulled a jar off a shelf.

Josh scowled at his sister. "I don't need her putting that stuff on me."

Marta couldn't help staring at Josh's back. She felt partly responsible for the bleeding red welts on his shoulder blades. What a shame. He had such nice shoulders and a beautiful tan that looked as if it had barely faded since summer. A wave of guilt washed over her. "I'll be glad to do it for you, Josh. You'll never be able to reach those cuts on your back." She stood and took the jar of salve from Ginny's hand. She could have sworn Josh flinched as she took a step toward him.

"OK, you two. I'm off to take my shower." Ginny twittered then winked at Marta on her way out of the room.

"What is she giggling about?"

"I have no idea," Marta answered, knowing full well the meaning of Ginny's innuendo. "Sit down and I'll take of those scratches for you."

"See if you can keep from ripping the rest of my hide off."

Marta held her hands under the warm water tap at the sink, opened the jar, and then dipped out some salve with her fingers. "I think we should call a truce . . . for Ginny's sake. After all, this is just a temporary arrangement."

"Just remember, you're on probation," he growled. "I'd do just about anything for my sister, but if there are any more incidents like what happened today, you'd better start packing your bags."

Marta rubbed some salve into Josh's shoulder. Immediately his muscles tensed under her fingers, but as she rubbed her hands over his back in circular motions, he began to relax. The heat from his body caused a faint, but pleasant herbal aroma to rise and tickle her nose. She kneaded the muscles on his shoulders and couldn't help but admire their broadness and strength. He didn't have an ounce of fat anywhere on him. No doubt all his hard physical labor kept him in such good shape. Would he get paunchy and bald as he got older? It would be a shame if all that wavy dark hair fell out someday.

She dipped out some more salve and worked it into his spine. He hadn't uttered a peep for several minutes. The herbs in the salve seemed to have a soothing effect on his injuries. Josh's eyelids dropped and his breathing slowed as the hardness of his muscles relaxed under her fingers. The refreshing oriental aroma of the herbs had a calming effect on her too, and she wasn't even the one receiving the backrub.

The sound of someone banging on the door caused Marta to reluctantly lift her hands from his tanned back. "I'll get it." She quickly washed the salve off her hands. "You'd better get a clean shirt on before you get a chill."

The banging continued, louder than before. Marta opened the door and found Miss Treymore preparing to whack the door with her cane. Her left arm was wrapped around a bulging grocery bag and she didn't look very happy.

"Why hello, Miss Treymore. Is there something we can help you with?"

"You can tell that landlord of ours to fix his doorbell. I've been standing out here in the cold for ages. I don't have time to stand around on his porch steps all day, you know. There's a special on the Discovery channel I want to watch. It's all about the demise of the buffalo. It's a shame what we did to those magnificent beasts. Though I can't say I'd turn down a nice warm buffalo robe, standing out in the cold like this."

"Would you like to come in?"

"Of course I want to come in. Did you think I climbed up these stairs just to keep my thighs in shape? If I want skinny thighs, all I have to do is sit on my sofa and exercise with that thingamajig that blond movie star on TV sells."

"You bought a-?"

"Of course I did. Bought a rowing machine too. It doesn't pay to let yourself go, you know. Anytime you want to borrow my exercise equipment, you just let me know. Now where's that landlord?"

Marta stepped aside to let the woman in, just as Josh walked in the room, buttoning a clean plaid flannel shirt. He stopped in the doorway when he saw who the visitor was.

"Is your garbage disposal acting up again?"

"No, it's working just fine since you fixed it." She set the brown paper bag on a chair and lifted out a paper plate covered in foil. "I brought you kids some cupcakes. You probably only eat the store bought kind, but I thought you should get a taste of my homemade ones." She pulled back a corner of the foil. "See. I decorated each one with an orange pumpkin face."

"That's very nice of you, Miss Treymore."

"Nice? That's all you've got to say? After I saved your life today and now I've brought you cupcakes made from my mother's own secret carrot cake recipe?"

"You didn't save my life."

"Sure she did," Marta quickly interrupted. "You were just too stunned to notice, that's all." She put her arm around the older woman's shoulders, giving her a quick hug.

43

Josh gave the two women a hard stare. "Thank you. For the cake." He rolled his eyes, "And for saving my life. Now, if that's all, I've got some things to tend to."

"That's not quite all Sonny. There's more in this bag." She pulled out a stack of magazines and handed them to Marta. "These fashion magazines have pictures of lots of pretty clothes. I thought you could look through them and get some ideas on how a young lady should dress."

Josh made a noise that sounded suspiciously like a snort. Marta didn't quite know what to say. The last thing she wanted to be reminded of was how short she came of being acceptable. Would she ever escape the stigma of being a foster kid? Not that Miss Treymore was trying to be unkind . . . she was just aiming to help and in the process, had hit a nerve.

"Marta is dressed just fine for the job she was doing."

Marta flashed a grateful smile toward Josh. She hadn't expected him to come to her defense. No matter, someday she would show Josh, Miss Treymore, and the whole world she could dress like a lady. A very well-to-do lady.

"Well, I'll leave you two to pour over your women's magazines. I need to get some plywood tacked up over a broken window before it rains."

Miss Treymore yanked a sheet of paper from the brown bag and shoved it under his nose. "Wait just a minute, sonny. I haven't told you the reason for my visit yet."

"Which would be?" He glanced at the paper before him, but didn't reach out and take it.

"I'm here to give you this list of requests from the tenant's association."

Josh's eyebrows shot up. "We don't have a tenant's association."

"We do now. And I'm the president."

"Why haven't I heard of this uh, group of yours before?"

"We never had need of one before."

44

"And you do now?" Josh frowned and rubbed his temple. "And if I don't comply with this list of demands, then what?"

"These aren't demands, they're suggestions."

Miss Treymore stood toe to toe with Josh. The disparity in ages, height, and physical makeup was all in Josh's favor. However, Marta sensed that Miss Treymore had the upper hand and the thought made her giggle.

"This is no laughing matter, Missy." Miss Treymore fixed her piercing blue eyes on Marta. "People have a right to have a say in how they live."

Josh took advantage of the fact Miss Treymore's attention was no longer riveted on him, and took a step back, nearly knocking over an end table. Miss Treymore's head whirled around with the speed of lightening and she pointed her cane right in the middle of his chest.

"Don't forget I was the first one who took a chance and rented from you. Nobody else wanted to live in a rat-infested building with gang pictures spray-painted everywhere. The whole thing should have been condemned." The tip of her cane made slow circles closer and closer to Josh's chest. She wrinkled her pointed nose and sniffed. "What is that funny smell? You haven't been smoking any of those illegal cigarettes have you?"

"There are no rats here, Miss Treymore. And no gangs either. I've seen to that. And that funny smell is some of Ginger's herbal rubbing liniment. You know very well I don't smoke or take drugs."

"Hummp. Well, that's why I took a chance on this place. No gangs and no rats. Now if you'd just read the list, you could make this place something people would be proud to live in. The tenant's association is not threatening a rent strike, or anything like that yet, but we want you to know we are serious about commencing a dialog between the landlord-that's you-and tenants."

Marta had to hand it to Josh. If he was losing his temper, which could be understandable, he sure didn't show it. In fact, he spoke to the old lady in a very gentle voice.

"Give me the list." He unfolded the paper, occasionally glancing at both women as he read.

Marta was dying to see the demands. "What does it say?" Josh didn't answer, but Marta could see the corners of his mouth twitching again. She wished she knew him well enough to know if it was a precursor to a smile, or if he was silently gnashing his teeth.

He finally spoke. "It says here, um, number one, you want me to change the name of the apartments to something elegant. Did you have something in mind?"

"Not yet. Do you want us to vote on it? It should be something classy . . . not just a jumble of buildings named after a street."

"Well, I think that is certainly negotiable. However, number two is not. I simply can't afford it."

"That's a shame. All the better apartments have recreation rooms. People need a place to gather for potlucks, parties and association meetings."

"I agree that would be nice, but if I built one, I'd have to raise everybody's rent. I want this place to be affordable. What is this third item? You want Marta to be the liaison when disputes arise?"

"That's right. When I told everyone how this poor little thing needs a job so badly, we thought it would make her more valuable to you if she had something important to do."

"And I don't suppose anyone would think of manufacturing disputes just so she'd have job security?" Josh's tone of voice hadn't changed, but his eyebrows were threatening to disappear into the deep wrinkles above his nose.

"And did Marta put you up to this?" He quit furrowing his brow long enough to cast a meaningful stare at Marta.

"Of course not! We wanted to surprise her."

Marta had kept her silence long enough. It was one thing for the renters to take over Josh's business, but no one was going to decide her future. She wasn't going to meet an abundance of rich men while she was blowing maple leaves to the end of the parking lot. In fact, the kind of man she was looking for would probably never even drive down the street out front, let alone feel compelled to stop and inspect the female in overalls.

"That's all very nice. But you see, I'm only here temporarily . . . just a couple of weeks, or a month at the most." Marta could have sworn Josh let out a sigh of relief.

"Look," he interrupted, "would you be satisfied if Marta worked with you on the rest of this list in her spare time?"

"That's all I asked for." Miss Treymore grinned in satisfaction and let the tip of her cane drop to the floor.

"Wait a minute, Josh. I don't remember giving you control of my spare time." Marta glared at Josh, who so cavalierly shoved his problem onto her. "I have a life of my own, and if you recall, I'll be spending any spare time looking for a real job."

"I meant," he said, in a tone reserved for talking to small children, "your spare time during the day when you're working for me. Any objections?"

"I guess not. Experience as a liaison in landlord-tenant disputes would certainly beef up my job resume. I assume I can count on you to write me a glowing letter of recommendation?"

"Are you suggesting your performance merits a recommendation?" Josh laughed for the first time that day. "From what I've seen so far, you'll be lucky if you don't leave here with a criminal record for assault and battery."

Marta took a deep breath, biting back the stinging retort she wanted to deliver. It wouldn't do to get into a full-blown argument in front of one of the tenants. If he couldn't take responsibility for his part in his accident, there

47

wasn't much for her to say, anyway. She was stuck, for the time being, with his arrogant attitude. But not for long.

"Miss Treymore spoke up, "I think I'll just leave these magazines here for you to look over, dear. I've already missed most of Wheel of Fortune. It's so important to keep using one's mind, you know. I can answer most of the questions long before the contestants, but once in a while, I have to look something up. Last week I had to take the bus to the library to find out the names of the presidents' wives. Of course, I knew most of them, but would you believe I couldn't remember the name of Harding's wife?"

"I'm sure it would have come to you if you'd thought about it long enough, Miss Treymore." Marta walked the woman to the door. "I'll look at your list and the magazines too, just as soon as I get a chance. Thank you so much for coming by."

"You're so welcome, dearie. It's going to be a pleasure working with you. I just knew the minute I met you, we were going to be good friends. With my help, I know you'll have that landlord whipped into shape in no time."

Marta waited till the tapping noise of Miss Treymore's cane reached the bottom step before she turned to face Josh. He was nowhere to be seen.

***

Josh stepped back from the window, satisfied the plywood sheet would keep out any rain until he could get new glass installed. One thing about physical labor, it went a long way toward venting frustration. Thanks to his new helper, he'd lost a half days work. He'd also lost time from work the day before when he'd stopped to clean up the paint mess in the kitchen. At this rate, he'd never get these apartments ready to rent. Vacant apartments were not going to pay the hefty mortgage he'd taken out on the place. Even with the government assistance he was getting for developing low-income housing, money was going to be tight for a while.

He could swing it though, if he didn't get sidetracked by any more incidents. All he had to do was keep a tight rein on Marta. She needed intense supervision and training, that was for sure. Willingness to work hard was a virtue he admired, since he demanded it in himself. So far, Marta showed the same quality. Whether she was careless or just accident prone, he didn't know yet, but either way, he wasn't going to take any more chances on her doing things her own way.

He'd also have to have a talk with Miss Treymore. She shouldn't be getting Marta sidetracked with all that fashion nonsense. Not that there was anything wrong with a woman looking nice. He liked a beautiful woman as much as the next guy. What he didn't like, were women who let the latest makeup and clothing fads take over their lives, at the expense of their inner beauty. Marta had a natural beauty. The beauty God gave her. She didn't need to be fiddling with it.

Josh wondered if his sister would learn something about constraint from Marta. When she enrolled in beauty school, he hoped she would gain self-confidence while she learned a trade. The first time she had come home after a classmate had experimented on Ginger's hair, he'd nearly yanked her out of that school. He hadn't, though. Ginger derived more pleasure from being a beautician than he'd ever thought possible. More importantly, she had stuck with it and now had a steady income. She had been drifting from job to job when he'd found her after all those years apart. Now they both had the stability that had been missing from their lives. Marta could have it too, if she'd follow his counsel.

The more Josh rolled the situation over in his mind, the more firmly convinced he was that he could provide Marta with the guidance she had so obviously been missing in her life. After all, it couldn't be much harder to mentor two women than one. Did she know the Lord? Ginger said she did, but if so, Marta was pretty quiet about it. She'd perk up after attending church with them a few times.

Maybe if she stayed, he could even talk her into giving him another backrub. Man, had her hands ever felt good when she massaged that herb stuff into his shoulders. He also admired the way she'd handled Miss Treymore. Yep. Marta definitely had a lot of potential. He put the tools away and headed to the apartment.

***

Marta assembled ingredients for a stew while Ginger put the rest of their grocery purchases away. Even though Ginger paid for her and Josh's share of the groceries, Marta had still shopped carefully, only selecting items that were nourishing, but inexpensive. Ginger had objected when Marta removed two frozen pizzas and a giant can of chili from the shopping cart. However when Marta had shown her the money she would save by buying the ingredients and cooking from scratch, she relented . . . as long as Marta agreed to do the majority of the cooking.

"Ginger, I've been thinking . . ." Marta seared the stew meat while her friend chopped potatoes, carrots and celery into bite size chunks. "When I get established, you and I should find an apartment nearer the city, or even over in Bellevue."

"What's wrong with this apartment? I'm getting it fixed up real nice." Ginger increased the tempo of her chopping.

"Oh, I didn't mean to imply it wasn't, Ginger. I just thought now that you've gained a little more experience, you could find a job in one of those upscale salons. Naturally you'd want to live close by." Marta crushed a clove of garlic and added it to the meat. The aroma filled the kitchen. "Wouldn't it be fun to be roommates on a long term basis?"

Ginger dropped the knife into the sink with a clatter. She scooped up the vegetables and dropped them into a bowl.

"Ginger?" Marta flinched when Ginger slammed the bowl down next to the stove. "Did I say something wrong? You'd like to share an apartment with me wouldn't you?"

"You may not have noticed, but we are sharing an apartment." Gingers voice sounded tight, as if she were speaking through clamped lips.

"Of course we-"

"No, Marta. I don't think it would be a good idea. Ever since you got here, you've acted like this place was beneath you. Like Josh and I were beneath you. All we've tried to do is help you. But you act like you can't wait to get away from us." Ginger choked off her last words and wiped a tear from her eye.

"Ginger, I'm-"

"Don't. Don't say you're sorry. It's plain that you and I don't have much in common anymore. Sure, I could move to a nicer apartment with you, but how long would that last? Till you find that rich husband you've been hoping for? What will I do then?"

Marta was genuinely distressed she'd hurt her friend's feelings but she wasn't sorry for trying to take control over her own destiny. "Ginger, wait. I didn't realize I was putting you down. I don't really think I'm better than you. But I have to set goals. I have to make a life for myself. A good life. I've never had that. Not a life of my own. Can't you please try and understand?"

"I understand perfectly. I hope your dreams all come true, Marta. However, you won't find true happiness till you let the Lord fully into your life."

Marta watched her friend disappear into the bedroom. The door shut behind her with a thunk of finality. Would she have to give up her best friend to get the things she craved? It wasn't a fair trade. There had to be a compromise. Maybe if she just quit talking to Ginger about her plans, it might help. But what fun were dreams if you didn't have anyone to share them with? They used to share everything . .

. clothes, homework, even once a candy bar they'd swiped from a foster mother's hidden stash.

And what did she mean about letting the Lord into her life? She'd been saved for years. She'd even attended church faithfully during the last year in Portland. It was the least she could do after Mona had rescued her from a life of living out of dumpsters. She had thanked God she'd never had to resort to anything illegal or immoral during that time. Panhandling was bad enough.

Many things had changed during the years Marta and Ginger had been apart, but there was still that bond between them. A bond too precious to sever. Marta poured liquid over the stew meat and added the vegetables. She wished she had some tarragon to add. Salt, pepper and garlic powder made up the extent of Ginger's spice cabinet. Cooking obviously wasn't a priority with Ginger. But what were the important things in her life? Had Marta stopped to ask? Had she forgotten friendship is a two-way street? Maybe Ginger had every right to be upset.

Marta set the table, not feeling very proud of her behavior toward Ginger, or even Josh. She found some old place mats and napkins and put them out. A dash outside yielded a bouquet of colorful maple leaves. The stew bubbled on the stove, sending an aroma that spoke of home cooking throughout the apartment. Maybe she hadn't been the best friend in the world, but at least she could show her appreciation in this small way. Marta hoped it wasn't too late to salvage her friendship with Ginger. When they were kids, they clung to each other out of need. Ginger obviously didn't need her anymore. She had Josh to fight her battles for her. As aggravating as Josh was, Marta could see he adored his sister and was committed to watching out for her. Their lives were already set on the path they'd chosen for themselves. Marta needed to get on with her own life. She could still be Ginger's friend, but when it came to her own future Marta had to depend on herself. Marta squared her shoulders in preparation for the challenge ahead.

CHAPTER FIVE

Josh finished the caulking around the bathtub. He enjoyed these quiet times working with his hands. He could talk to the Lord and even sing praise songs out loud. He let out a satisfied sigh, glad to be done with the last of the bathrooms in building number three. New renters were already making plans to move in. Thanks to Marta.

He never would have believed just a week ago, how indispensable she could be. She had totally taken over showing the newly remodeled apartments and checking the prospective renters' references. And it had only taken her two meetings with the newly formed tenants' association to satisfy their demands without costing him an arm and leg. They had collectively come up with a name for the apartments . . . Maple Vista Apartments. Who would have thought a name would be so important to the occupants of his apartment building? He also never would have predicted the satisfaction he felt when he put up the new sign out front, but he did. All due to the woman he had once been ready to put out on the street.

A rush of tenderness for his new helper filled him. She tried hard to please. Even when she disagreed with him, which was often, he only had to think of the home cooked meals she prepared every night, and he didn't allow the disagreement to disintegrate into an argument. Admittedly, it wasn't easy sometimes. He was used to having his own way. However, when faced with the decision of wasting time and money planting tulips bulbs in front of each apartment in order to have a scrumptious meal of chicken and dumplings, his growling stomach settled it. The promise of pot roast, mashed potatoes and gravy helped him decide to paint the apartment interiors a soft white instead of the bright white he had originally planned.

If the truth were known, he enjoyed sitting in the kitchen just before dinner and watching Marta prepare the meal. The first time he'd sat there mesmerized like that, watching her stick a fork in the roast to test its doneness, he'd almost scalded himself with hot coffee. Brewed coffee, not instant. Made by Marta. How had he gotten along before she arrived? What could he do to keep her around?

For starters, he'd give her a raise. He couldn't afford to give her much, but she'd earned a higher wage. She had taken over almost all matters concerning the tenants, leaving him time to do the things he liked best . . . fixing up the buildings. After that first day, he'd learned to be careful about the jobs he gave her. No more jobs that entailed working machinery, or coming in contact with cleaning solvents or paint. Not that she wasn't willing. He just valued his life too much, and hers, to take a chance of bodily injury.

Josh grinned. Marta still wore those overalls he'd bought her. Yesterday she'd added a colored scarf and he noticed she had embroidered "MVA" on the pocket, for Maple Vista Apartments. She must like it here as much as he did. Winter was coming on. He'd get her some boots and a heavy raincoat. She'd need it when she was making the rounds of the parking lots to check if everyone was in their proper stalls. Maybe he should get her a pair of fleece-lined boots. No sense in taking a chance of her getting cold.

Josh took one last look around the vacant apartment. Satisfied it was ready to rent, he let himself out and ambled across the lawn to his tool shed. A UPS truck pulled up in front of his apartment. He was expecting a package from a plumbing supply warehouse, so he walked over to the curb.

"I've got a delivery for Marta Petrosky."

"She's around back right now. I'll sign for it." Josh scribbled his name on the receiving ticket and wondered what Marta had ordered. He'd cautioned her about spending too much time watching the shopping channel with Miss Treymore, but she might have let herself be talked into buying a little trinket from there anyway. The UPS driver disappeared into his truck and then come out carrying two huge boxes. *This is no little trinket.*

54

"Where do you want me to put these?"

"I guess you'd better bring them inside." Josh led the way to their apartment and opened the door. "Just set them on the floor."

"If you could hold the door open while I bring in the rest, I'd appreciate it."

"The rest?" He shifted his weight from one foot to the other as the driver brought out several more boxes. Each box was big enough to hold a small TV set. What was all this stuff? And where did she think she was going to store it? Nothing on the outside of the boxes gave any indication which store they came from. They were just plain packing boxes. Twelve of them. And the UPS truck was still parked at the curb.

"Could you give me a hand?"

"Are you sure you've got the right Marta Petrosky? I'd hate to have to haul all this stuff back onto the truck." Josh felt his jaw drop as the driver struggled to drag a steamer trunk to the sidewalk.

"I'm sure. I double checked the address. Marta Petrosky. In care of Ginger Morton. Are you Mr. Morton?"

"Unfortunately, I am." Josh was beginning to regret his foolish assumption that everything in his life was starting to go smoothly. Marta's delivery was spread over half the floor of the small living room. Even if she lived in the apartment alone, there wouldn't have been enough closet space to accommodate it all. Things were already cramped. What could she have been thinking to have ordered all this?

"I hope this trunk is the last of it." Josh grunted as he set down his end of the huge storage chest. He straightened up, grateful the weight of it hadn't thrown his back out.

"Yep. That's about it. Except for one more thing."

The driver ducked back into the truck and came out with a manila envelope. Josh was so thankful it wasn't another trunk, he briefly considered hugging the guy before he left. Josh firmly shut the door and glared at Marta's boxes.

***

Marta let herself out Miss Treymore's front door. She'd spent an hour trying to convince the older lady Josh's responsibility did not include replacing light bulbs inside the apartments. Now she would be late starting dinner. It was only going to be spaghetti, but she liked to simmer the sauce for a while before serving. Mona Von Cleef had shared her special sauce recipe with Marta before she passed away. A pinch of cinnamon just before serving pulled all the other flavors together. Josh and Ginger would love it.

Marta glanced at her watch, and realized Ginger might be home already. She hoped Ginger hadn't decided to start dinner on her own. It would most likely come from a can, and bound to be ruined. Josh was paranoid about dead batteries in all the smoke alarms and Marta sympathized. Almost every pot and pan in Ginger's cupboard looked as if someone had scorched food in it. But that was just Ginger. There wasn't a person in the world more loyal or had a bigger heart than Ginger's, so blackened pots were something Marta could overlook.

Ginger stood on the doorstep, waving her arms and beckoning Marta to hurry. *Uh, oh. She looks a little frazzled. I wonder if I've done something to make Josh angry again.* Marta quickened her pace and darted into the living room right behind Ginger. Her toe stubbed against something and her forward motion caused her to sprawl face down on a pile of cartons.

"Marta! Are you ok? Didn't you see those boxes there? You ran right into them."

Marta groaned and pushed herself up to a kneeling position. She imagined her lower legs were going to be a mass of bruises but she didn't think anything was broken. Well, maybe her face was broken. She gingerly ran her fingertips across her right cheekbone. She could feel a raised welt, but at least when she lowered her hand it wasn't covered in blood. Of course, broken bones weren't always

56

accompanied by bleeding. Broken bones did cause disfigurement, though. And pain. "Ohhhhhhhh."

"Here. Let me help you up. Can you walk?"

Marta let Ginger help her to her feet. Her face throbbed and it hurt to open her mouth. She made a solemn promise to herself that as soon as she could talk, somebody was going to get a tongue lashing for booby trapping the living room. Picking her way through the maze in the room would be a challenge, but she felt the need to sit down. By the time she made it to the tattered plaid recliner, Ginger reached her side with a wet cloth.

"Here. I put some ice in this. I'm afraid you're still going to have a shiner, though."

"That's just great. My face has returned to normal after that allergic reaction and now I'm going to look like a prize fighter. I'll never get as far as an interview for a job at this rate." Marta reached for the wet cloth and held it to her face. The coolness felt good against her injury. "Thanks, Ginger."

"You're welcome. I'm glad you're not hurt bad. What are all these boxes anyway?"

"They're not yours? They must be Josh's then." Boy was he going to get a piece of her mind when he got home. Sure. It was his apartment building. But they all shared this little apartment. He should be more considerate. With all the vacant apartments he owned, there was no reason to use their living room for storage. "Is he home yet?"

"I haven't seen him. He'll be here soon, though. I heard him say this morning how much he was looking forward to dinner."

"Dinner!" Marta stood, wincing with pain at the sudden movement. "I've got to get started. I haven't even browned the hamburger yet." She hurried to the kitchen, grabbing things from the shelves as she moved around assembling the necessary ingredients. The only time she stopped was to hold the makeshift icepack up to her face. Thank goodness she and Ginger had fallen into a routine. They made a good team in the kitchen as long as Ginger kept her mind on what she was doing.

"Something smells good."

Josh's deep voice interrupted Marta's thoughts. She kept on chopping onions and kept her face averted. There was plenty of time for Josh to see the results of his actions when they all sat down to eat. Instead of going in to shower like he usually did though, he hovered around her. She could sense his presence behind her . . . feel his breath on her neck.

"This came for you today."

Marta ignored his touch on her arm and continued chopping.

"I'm assuming it's a packing slip or invoice for all that stuff you ordered. You'd better put it someplace safe."

Marta didn't like the tone of his voice at all. It sounded . . . accusatory. He was the one who should be on the defensive, not her.

"I don't know what you mean. I didn't order anything."

"Well, now. I wonder why your name is printed on this envelope and all those boxes in the other room."

Marta whipped her head around, causing a new wave of pain to stab through her cheekbone. "Let me see that." She held out her hand to receive the envelope.

"Hey. You've got quite a shiner developing there." Josh brought his face close to hers. Too close for her comfort. "Been wrestling with my ladder again?"

"Very funny!" She snatched the envelope from his hand. Aware of two pairs of curious eyes on her, she quickly skimmed the letter inside. "It's from my former employer. He says my things were returned to his house by the bus company."

"You brought all this stuff on the bus with you?" Josh's tone insinuated she had done something stupid. Again.

"No. I only had two boxes. Just a minute, let me read the rest." She frowned, trying to make sense of the rest of the letter. "I can't believe this."

"What?" Josh and Ginger spoke in unison.

"It says Mona wanted me to have all her things after she died since she never had a daughter. He apologizes for not sending them sooner, but he just couldn't bear to go through everything before. He says if I don't want them, I can give them to charity, but he hopes I'll use and enjoy everything." Marta laid the letter aside and read the second sheet. "There's even an inventory of what he sent. It's all her designer clothing and jewelry and some other things. I didn't expect this. Any of it."

Marta's throat tightened and tears threatened to start as she remembered her last days with Mona. The woman had literally taken her off the streets, brought her home and treated her as a member of her own family. She was the closest thing to a mother that Marta had ever known. Her husband had been kind too. Never treating her like a servant even though in reality she was. For over a year, she was a paid companion and caregiver to the dying woman. It was in the Von Cleef home where she learned what it meant to have fine things and respect.

"Cool! Let's open the boxes." Ginger started toward the living room, but Marta stopped her.

"Not yet, Ginger. I need time to absorb this. It was such a kind gesture, but I don't know if I'm ready to go through her things." Marta sniffed, her eyes watering more now. "These darned onions. I'd better put them in the skillet."

***

Josh sank into his recliner with the evening paper on his lap. A full stomach after working hard all day was all a man could ask for. He'd had that and more. A cup of freshly brewed coffee and a warm piece of apple pie rested on the table at his right elbow. He could get used to this. It made the small irritations of a day disappear pretty quickly.

He took a bite of pie and let it roll around his tongue. When had Marta found time to bake? This was no frozen desert. Nothing from the grocery store had ever tasted this good. The same could be said for the spaghetti and garlic bread she'd served for dinner. He was going to have to watch his waistline if she kept this up. Small price to pay for home cooked meals, though. Not that he couldn't cook if he put his hand to it, but when had he had time recently? This new arrangement was working out perfectly.

Josh tried to concentrate on the sports page, but his sister's giggles and occasional bursts of laughter from the other room, made it hard. What were those two up to anyway? Probably going through those boxes. They had dragged some of them into their bedroom right after dinner. Ginger was supposed to be washing the dishes but got sidetracked with helping Marta. Maybe he should do the dishes. It was the least he could do after Marta had worked so hard to get the meal on the table. He scraped the last bite of pie from the plate and licked his fork clean. If he did the dishes, no one would blame him if he cut himself another piece of pie, either. He drank the last of his coffee, stood and headed for the kitchen.

Even the sound of running water didn't drown out The women's voices. If anything, he could hear them better in the kitchen. What were they doing? Josh finished scrapping the plates, not that there was any food left on them, but it was a routine he'd gotten into over the years. He ran hot water in one side of the double sink and watched the bubbles rise after he squirted some dishwashing liquid in the water. At least the hot water tank was working. He yanked his hand out of the scalding water. Someone could get badly burned doing this. As soon as he found time, he'd repair the built-in dishwasher.

The bedroom door clicked open and the sound of more boxes being shoved around caught his attention. "What are you gals doing?"

"Marta's looking for the box with her own clothes in it. She's sorting the other things into piles and I'm trying to talk her into trying some of them on." Ginger peered around the corner where Josh was putting the last of the dishes back in the cupboard. "Oh Josh, I'm sorry. It was my turn to clean up tonight."

"That's ok. It sounded like you two are having too much fun to stop. You can take my turn tomorrow night." Josh accepted a hug from his sister and thought how lucky he was to have her back in his life. Her effusiveness never failed to make him smile. Ginger bounced out of the kitchen and he tried to remember a time when he had felt this content. "Hey," he hollered out, "There wouldn't be any rain gear in those boxes by any chance, would there?"

Muffled giggling erupted from behind the closed bedroom door again. Ginger opened it a crack and peeked out.

"No. But we could really use a man's opinion. I think these things are way too old fashioned."

"There *not* old-fashioned, Ginger." Marta voice sounded defensive. "These are classic designs. And very expensive. Most of them have never even been worn because Mona stayed in her dressing gown the last few months. I remember her husband ordering a whole bunch of these things from New York. He kept telling her she was going to get well and could wear them then."

Ginger opened the door wider. "Classic, as in boring. Take a look, Josh."

Josh really didn't want to be drawn into an argument between the two women. One of them would get mad at him for sure. He looked anyway. Marta was not wearing the new coveralls he had bought her. She was wearing a black dress. He sucked in his breath. The dress looked more like a slip. Little straps over the shoulders and some kind of shiny beads just below the low neckline. He had a sudden urge for a drink of water. If the way that dress hugged Marta's curves, all the way down to her knees, was old-fashioned, then someone had better redefine the term.

"Well?" Ginger put her hands on her hips and looked to Josh for an opinion.

He couldn't stop staring at Marta. His gaze dropped to the hemline and the gorgeously shaped legs below. How did women stand to wear those high heels, anyway? How did they keep them on to walk? There were only a couple of little straps holding them on. He looked back at her face. Her eyes shone . . . as if wearing that dress was a gift she had been waiting for. As if she'd never worn anything nice before.

"Uh. It's very pretty." Josh stumbled over the words, not knowing how to tell her she was drop-dead gorgeous. "I don't know if it's very practical for wearing around here, though."

"Silly." Marta laughed, making her even more beautiful. "This is a cocktail dress. It's for wearing to parties, or other evenings out."

Josh wondered what parties she was referring to. Surely she didn't mean she was going out on dates? If she did, would she wear her hair pinned up like that? He'd better tell her it wouldn't be a good idea. It left that soft spot below her ear exposed and someone might take advantage and try and kiss her there. Still, what else could she mean? He'd never seen anyone dressed like that at a Seahawks game.

"I knew that." *Over my dead body. You don't even know anyone in this town. I'm not about to let you parade around where some creep can look down your dress.*

"I should have known my brother would be swayed by that dress." Ginger didn't sound too unhappy that Josh had sided with Marta. "I guess I should have had you give an opinion on some of the other outfits."

Josh patted Ginger's shoulder, and took one last look at Marta before he turned to leave the room. "I'm going to relax in my chair. I've not adverse to you bringing your fashion show into the living room, however." He smiled at the thought of Marta trying on all the dresses that must be packed in the boxes and parading through the house for him to admire. Yep, he'd better sit in the chair and center his attention on reading the paper. No sense letting her know she was having this effect on him. In fact, he'd better lighten things up. He looked over his shoulder and winked. "In fact, I'd be glad to give an opinion on which colors look best with that black eye of yours."

"Come on Josh! Would it kill ya to be nice?"

Ginger gave him a shove before slamming the door behind him. He escaped back to his chair, away from that tiny room. Away from Marta, whose perfume still filled his nostrils. When had she started wearing that scent? It smelled expensive. And desirable as anything he'd ever smelled. Josh rattled the paper and tried to focus on the football scores. A thump sounded from the other room and intruded on his concentration. What was Marta wearing now? Darn it, a woman who cooked like her had no right to look like that too. He had just begun getting comfortable having her around and now she had to go and do this. He didn't like it. Not one bit.

He looked up from the paper. The door was still closed. Were they going to stay in there all night? Josh tried to calculate how long it would take to go through all those boxes. Probably forever if they were full of clothes and Marta tried everything on. Maybe he should offer to cart some of the boxes into the bedroom. He might as well. They made it impossible for him to enjoy a relaxing evening in his chair.

Josh put down his newspaper and slammed the recliner's foot rest back down. He always had to give it a good kick to get the chair into its full upright position. Ginger had been after him to get a new chair, but he was used to this one. Why get rid of a perfectly good chair and get one that may not be as snug? Who cared if it was ugly and got stuck half the time. It would probably last another five years.

He was able to lift three of the boxes since they weren't heavy. He couldn't very well tap on the door with his hand, so used his toe. The door open and peeked around his load to see Marta standing there.

"Here. Let me take one of those." She lifted the top one off the stack he was holding and set it on the bed.

Josh's heart filled with disappointment to see Marta was no longer wearing the black dress. Instead she had on some kind of jogging suit that zipped up the front, all the way to her chin. She looked pretty in that light purple color. But then, she looked good in anything he'd seen her in so far.

Ginger exploded into his view. "So, what do ya think? Would I make a great society babe, or what?" She pirouetted around the room showing off a floor length blue dress. Somehow it didn't look very elegant on her since she was a full head shorter than Marta. The sleek style of the dress presented a direct contrast to Ginger's wild looking hair and makeup. "You look really cute, honey." Josh dropped his packages on the bed next to the others. "The guys at the country club will be fighting over who gets to dance with you."

"Yeh, right. As if I'd be caught dead at any country club. But Marta would fit right in."

CHAPTER SIX

Marta slowly slid her fingers over the soft wool blazer, turning from side to side in front of the mirror. No one would say she came from the wrong side of the tracks if they could see her now. If it wasn't for her unruly long hair, she wouldn't have recognized herself. She'd have to do something about the hair. A classic page boy was just what her new look called for. It would require cutting off at least ten inches but Ginger would do it for her. Ginger would be thrilled to have a chance at Marta's hair. She'd offered her hairdressing skills to Marta several times. Marta was sure there wasn't much Ginger could do to ruin it as long as she didn't color it or insist on a perm.

She lifted a single strand of pearls to her throat. They were perfect, down to the tiny diamond clasp. Were the pearls synthetic? Probably not. Like everything else Mona had owned, they represented the best money could buy. Marta turned again, admiring the matching pleated wool skirt. The hem hit her just below the knee. She loved the understated, but rich look of the suit. It would be perfect to wear when she finally got a job in the front office of a . . . a what? Where did she really want to work? Closing her eyes, she pictured what the office would look like. Plush carpets and walnut paneling came to mind. But as for the job itself? She really couldn't think of anything she'd like to do. Plus . . . she didn't have the most impressive resume.

A noise from the other side of the bedroom door caught Marta's attention. Josh must be back from the hardware store. The back of his old pickup would probably be filled with building materials. While he was perfectly capable of unloading everything himself, she was determined to make herself useful. She quickly slipped out of the designer clothes, carefully hanging them away on the padded hangers Mona's husband had sent along. Ginger had generously given up part of her half of the closet space. Bless Ginger.

Even Josh had offered to store the summer things in his own room. Her appreciation for him had grown. She sometimes had thoughts that Ginger was lucky to have an older brother like him watching out for her. However, most of the time, good sense prevailed and Marta saw Josh's overprotectiveness and bossiness as a negative thing. Ginger would never mature as an adult as long as she depended on Josh for everything. In the two weeks she had lived with them, Marta had never heard of Ginger mention any close friends. She'd never gone out in the evening, preferring instead, to stay at home with Josh and Marta. Ginger was twenty-three, only a year younger than Marta. She needed a social life.

Marta quickly pulled on the coveralls she'd worn that morning. She might as well get as much use out of them as she could. Admittedly, they were more comfortable and practical for working around the apartments than anything else she had. The new wardrobe would be used soon enough, when she started job hunting in earnest. It wouldn't be long now and she'd be on her way.

Just as Marta expected, Josh was busy putting his purchases away in the shed. He whistled an unfamiliar but upbeat tune. She hurried over to the truck and picked up two paper bags. "Whoa. What are in these? They're heavy."

"Roofing nails. Watch out you don't poke your fingers on them. The clerk didn't double-bag them when I checked out."

"I'll be careful." Indeed, since her first catastrophic week on the job, she had gone out of her way to avoid any more unpleasant incidents. Sometimes it wasn't easy to concentrate, though, because Josh had a tendency to hover. She caught him staring at her on more than one occasion while she worked. Well, at least he didn't glower as much. In fact he had an attractive twinkle in his eye most of the time. Had he changed? Or had she merely gotten used to him?

66

He was scrutinizing her now. When those marble blue eyes turned her way, she felt awkward and clumsy. As if to prove a point to herself, she stubbed her toe and pitched forward, nearly losing her grip on the nails. At least she managed to keep her footing this time. No thanks to Josh. What was he looking at, anyway? She quickly looked down to make sure her zipper hadn't come undone. Satisfied she hadn't invited his inspection, she met his gaze head-on.

"If you're waiting for me to fall flat on my face, you're wasting your time. I worked all morning clearing the debris from last night's rain storm off the parking lots and sidewalks. Even I couldn't find anything to trip over now."

"I see that. Nice job." Josh turned a huge smile on her, showing a row of dazzlingly white teeth. Marta liked the way deep lines formed in his face when he smiled like that. Unlike many men she had met, Josh's expression was usually open and totally lacking in artifice. There was little he kept hidden. Unlike her. She was hiding a lot.

She ducked her head, lowering her lashes, as if the act kept her thoughts from him. Was Ginger right? Would Josh be angry with her if she told him her plans? Well, no sense tempting fate. She'd keep the information to herself. It wasn't any of Josh's business anyway. Besides, it was bad enough she had to tiptoe around the subject with Ginger these days. Even though Ginger had genuinely been excited over Marta's good fortune in receiving Mona's things, Ginger had deep reservations about her plans. To her credit, she had never mentioned it to Marta again after that one flare up.

"What are you thinking about? You're off in another world." Josh's voice reflected his smile.

"Oh, nothing you'd be interested in." *Or anything I'd care to share.*

Josh stepped toward her and took the bundles of nails from her arms. Instead of stepping away, he looked her full in the eyes. "You might be surprised what I'm interested in."

67

He stood close enough that Marta could almost make out each individual whisker on his chin. His beard certainly grew fast even though she knew he shaved closely each morning. She caught a faint whiff of the spicy aftershave he used. By afternoon, though, he always looked as if he could use another shave. How prickly would it feel if she lifted her hand to his face? She barely lifted her hand, then dropped it. What in the world had she been thinking? She didn't want to touch Josh. What if Miss Treymore or someone else came by and got the wrong idea?

Marta took a quick step backward. "I was just wondering why Miss Treymore stands by her window each day to wait for the mail."

"Why don't you ask her? You two have gotten pretty close." Josh brushed past her and headed toward his truck.

Marta wasn't surprised when Josh didn't offer an opinion. Men were pretty dense when it came to discerning other people's behavior. Just like now. All she had to do was offer a simple explanation for her actions and he just accepted it at face value. He didn't know he made her slightly uncomfortable when he stood so close and she wasn't about to tell him. He'd only use the information to tease her and get in her space at every opportunity. Just to see her squirm. She didn't want to start that kind of game with him. Not when they were just falling into a comfortable routine.

She helped him finish unloading the truck, aware he continued to scrutinize her every move. What was that man's problem? Marta sent him a tentative smile. His answering wink dispelled the notion he might be waiting to pounce on her for her making a mistake. No. It was more as if he were almost . . . leering. Josh? Leering? Nah. If anything, he treated her like a little sister. Just like he treated Ginger. All her preening in the mirror earlier must be giving her a big head.

To Marta's relief, Josh's voice finally broke into her thoughts. "I think we're through here for the day. Are there any issues with the tenants I should be aware of?"

"Everybody's happy. Two families will be moving in this weekend. An older couple and a young couple with a baby. I'm waiting to hear back on the reference checks on the other couple."

"Good work. Why don't you take the rest of the day off?"

Marta didn't have to be persuaded. The want ad section of the newspaper was lying on her bed and she happily anticipated lining up interviews. "Thanks, Josh. I think I'll drop by Miss Treyemore's for a little while and then I'll be in the apartment if you need me." She turned away from Josh and his watchful eyes. If he saw her skipping down the sidewalk away from him and concluded she was happy to go, she didn't care. She'd worked hard all week and deserved an afternoon to herself.

***

Josh stared after her as Marta bounced away from him. He'd almost given her something else to do, just so he could enjoy looking at her. Her face had been all rosy from the cold and now that she had disappeared, the rosiness was gone as well. Dark clouds hovered overhead and a cold breeze sprang up, reminding him winter was just around the corner. It was past time to get the roof repaired on the last building. He'd better get cracking if he wanted to beat the next rain storm.

He spent the rest of the afternoon taking up old asphalt shingles and replacing them with new ones. The roof probably needed replacing, but that would have to wait a couple of years. In the meantime, the repairs would keep any rain from further damaging the structure underneath. Tomorrow he'd take down the old cracked wooden gutters and replace them with new aluminum ones. Once he got this done, he could look forward to starting the inside work.

Work he didn't have to do alone because Marta would be at his side.

Marta seemed eager to get away today. It didn't take a genius to figure out she probably was anxious to get back to the apartment to start dinner. Every meal she'd prepared was a tribute to her cooking skills. Nobody could cook like that unless they really loved doing it. Josh knew how lucky he was to be a recipient of that care. He must remember to *always* show his appreciation. Anything to keep those meals coming. Maybe he should consider buying her a couple of those fancy pans Miss Treymore said were advertised on the shopping channel. The value of good tools in his job were no more important than the proper kitchen tools. If Marta had better cooking utensils, who knows what wonderful things she'd make?

Ginger was already home when Josh arrived. She stood at the counter peeling the cellophane from a grocery store pizza. Pizza? They hadn't eaten that in almost two weeks. He rubbed his hand over his sternum. He couldn't say he had missed it, or the heartburn it usually caused. Where was the home cooked meal he'd been expecting? Ok, maybe he'd been taking things for granted, but Marta liked cooking. Didn't she? Josh looked around but didn't see any sign of her.

"Is that dinner?"

His sister directed the same proud smile at him that she'd smiled when she had shown him the frog she'd caught fifteen years ago. "It sure is. I figured it was about time I took my turn at it."

Josh swallowed his frustration. "I hadn't realized you two were taking turns."

"It was my idea. Marta insisted it was her job, since she had more time than us, but she's been pretty busy today, so I offered. Do you have a problem with that, dear brother?"

There were times when it didn't pay to tell the truth and Josh figured this was one of them. He'd already spent too many evenings in his life eating takeout food. He'd spent even more evenings alone. Neither prospect was one he wanted to repeat. Tonight's dinner reminded him of the thought he'd entertained earlier . . . buying Marta some fancy pots and pans. He didn't care what it cost. It would be his birthday present to himself. Maybe the last five birthdays. Whatever it took.

"No problem at all, Ginny. I think I'll go clean up while I'm waiting." On the way to the shower, he headed to his bedroom for clean clothes. The other bedroom door was standing wide open and he could easily see Marta bent over the newspaper with a pen in hand. He paused, admiring the thick shiny curls cascading over her shoulders. He felt like a voyeur, so cleared his throat.

Marta barely glanced at him. "Oh. Hi, Josh."

Ok, so she wasn't thrilled to see him peeking through her door. How hard would it have been for her to at least send him one of her beautiful smiles? She was certainly absorbed in whatever it was she was reading. Garage sale listings maybe? Or . . . was she still looking for a job? The thought made his stomach tighten. Right after he ate, he was going to take himself to Miss Treymore's place to get some advice on new things for the kitchen. Marta would be obligated to stay after she received such a practical gift from him.

He still thought of her as he stood under the hot spray in the shower. Perhaps obligated was not the reaction he wanted from Marta. He wanted her to want to stay. Because she was happy, not because she felt a duty to do so. Evidently she wasn't as happy as he'd thought or she wouldn't be going through the paper so intently. He rinsed the soap out of his hair and turned off the water. Wrapping a bath towel around his waist, he turned to the sink and reached for his razor.

***

Marta cringed each time a hunk of her hair fell to the floor. She wished there were a mirror in the kitchen so she could see what Ginger was doing. Perhaps it had been a mistake to trust Ginger to help her with a make-over.

"Stop fidgeting and wiggling around, Marta. Do you want me to whack off more than we agreed on?"

"Of course not!" Marta's voice sounded high pitched and scratchy to her own ears. Ginger must think she acted like a big baby. Getting a haircut was no big deal to Ginger. Probably no big deal to most people. But to her, it was. I had to come out perfect. She'd even cut some pictures out of an old mail-order catalog for Ginger to study before she started cutting.

"I really think I could copy the style you want better if you'd let me straighten your hair."

Marta flinched again as the noise of the scissors moved closer to her right ear. "No. Absolutely not. I don't want any chemicals put on my head. Remember the monster I turned into when I used those cleaning products? I'll just have to use a curling iron to straighten it."

"I remember. It's too bad. Some red highlights would really be pretty, though."

Marta reached up to feel the length of her hair.

"Marta! Please sit still."

"Couldn't I just go look in the mirror? Just to make sure I've given you the right pictures to look at?"

"Oh, all right. But hurry up."

Marta could hear Ginger chuckling in the background as she raced to the mirror in the bathroom. Feeling somewhat irritated that Ginger wasn't taking this haircut seriously she switched on the light and snatched up the hand mirror so she could view the back. Relief flooded through her when she saw her hair was shaping up exactly as she'd requested. She hurried back to the kitchen and sat in the chair. Ginger had swept up most of the shorn locks so at least she didn't have the growing pile of her hair to stare at in alarm anymore.

"Well? Are you going to tell me I butchered you?"

"No. Of course not. I just needed to check on the length." Marta relaxed and closed her eyes. "In fact, you're doing a wonderful job, Ginger. The style looks almost exactly like Mona's did."

"You're trying to look like Mona? Marta, what's wrong with looking like yourself? That is just too weird."

"What's weird?"

"Trying to look like a dead woman. You can't *be* her, Marta. You shouldn't even try." Ginger removed the protective cape from Marta's shoulders. "There, I'm all done."

Marta stood and brushed the remnants of deep brown curls from her lap. Ginger would never understand. There was no point in trying to explain how elegant Mona had always looked and how much all her friends loved and respected her. She shook her head and ran her fingers through her hair. Her head felt as if a giant weight had been removed. She turned and hugged her friend.

"Thank you so much, Ginger. It's perfect. Just what I wanted."

Ginger giggled. "Admit it, Marta." She gave her a playful slap on the shoulder. "You were scared to death I'd turn you into some kind of freak."

"I was not." Marta denied, trying to sound as convincing as possible. "I was just a little nervous, that's all. It's been a long time since I've had my hair cut."

Ginger's smile widened. "Protest all you want, Marta. I know you thought you were going to end up looking like my twin." She swept the last of Marta's hair into a dustpan. "I'm glad you're happy with it, though."

"I think I'll see how it looks with one of the new dresses. Maybe I'll try on that royal blue cashmere with the straight skirt and cowl neckline. And remember that kettle-brim hat? I'm going to try on a few more things."

"Too bad my brother's not home. I think he enjoyed that first fashion show you put on for him."

"I did not do that for him!" Marta automatically protested before she even realized Ginger was smirking. "I merely wanted to hear a man's point of view." Dang it anyway, did Ginger have to see an ulterior motive in everything? "Where is Josh, anyway? He disappeared right after dinner and didn't say where he was going."

"I think he said something about visiting Miss Treymore." Ginger went to the window and pulled back the gold curtain. "His truck is still out front."

Marta headed for the bedroom, but glanced back over her shoulder. "I've been meaning to ask you, Ginger . . . Do you think Miss Treymore has a crush on the mailman?"

"Wouldn't that be a hoot? He won't have a chance if she sets her mind to snaring him."

Marta thought about Ginger's statement. She truly liked both of the old folks. They seemed lonely. She pulled open the closet door and called out, "Maybe we can give them a little push in the right direction." The blue dress was gorgeous, All right. Marta slipped out of her clothes, pulled the dress over her head and smoothed the soft fabric down over her hips. A pair of high-heeled pumps and just the right accessories would complete the effect.

While she put on a pair of gold hoop earrings, the front door opened, announcing Josh's return. He spoke to Ginger and he sounded very pleased with himself about something. Ginger laughed and mumbled something Marta couldn't discern. Marta smiled to herself. Ginger was happy, Josh was happy and she was glad. Contentment was something none of them had experienced often enough.

"Marta, come on out and show Josh your hair cut." Ginger hollered out.

Oh great. Now if she didn't go out there, it would look as if something was wrong. If she did go out there, she'd end up standing in front of Josh waiting for his approval. Well, she looked pretty good, if she did say so herself. She was proud of her new image. She hadn't come this far so she could hide out in the bedroom. On the contrary. Marta ran the brush through her hair one more time, taking care that the ends curled slightly under. Then she opened the door and stepped out into the hall.

The first thing she saw as she entered the living room was Josh's expectant face turned toward her. His smile faded as she took a few steps closer to stand directly in front of him. Not the reaction she expected. He wasn't supposed to go from a friendly cocker spaniel, to a mean looking Rottweiler, in the space of three seconds. Where was the nod of approval she expected?

"I take it you don't like my new look." She didn't know why his blessing was so important, but suddenly it was. Maybe he just needed a few minutes to get used to it.

Josh's answer was clipped. "It doesn't look like you."

"Well pardon me for wanting to change." She saw she wasn't going to get his endorsement. Couldn't he at least be polite?

"Change? To what? This doesn't even look like you. You look like a stranger."

Marta puzzled over his reaction. Was he one of those men who had a thing about long hair? Or was it her makeup he didn't like? She glanced at Ginger for some indication of what Josh's problem was. Ginger merely looked away. She was certainly a big help. Had she known Josh would act this way? If so, why had she called her to the living room?

"Maybe you're only now seeing the real me."

"If this is the real you, I'm not sure I care for it. You sure don't need to get all dolled up to impress me or Ginger. So what's this all about?"

"I told you I was going to look for an office job. You even encouraged me."

"That was before-." Josh's mouth briefly clamped into a hard, straight line. "Is that what you really want?"

"Of course it is. I've said it over and over, haven't I?" Just let him deny it. He was as anxious for her to leave as she was to go. Heaven knows, he'd be glad to get his closet back. And if he wasn't paying her, he could hire a *real* helper as his assistant. He should be relieved she wouldn't be taking charity from him anymore. She took a deep breath and prepared to tell him how mean he was being.

"Ok, you look nice. Is that what you wanted to hear?" He grabbed his jacket from the chair. "I'm going out for a while."

Marta clamped her arms close to her chest as the door closed behind him. His behavior hurt. The sudden tears pooling in her eyes made her angry. Who cared what he thought, anyway? His views of her meant nothing. He was, after all, a flannel shirt, blue jean wearing, dumb jock who wouldn't know class if it bit him on the nose.

"I'm sorry, Marta. I don't know what got into him."

"That's all right, Ginger. I didn't expect anything different from him. After all, they don't exactly teach good manners in juvenile hall."

"That's not fair, Marta. Josh is slow to come around sometimes, that's all. I'm sure he's sorry for what he said."

"Well, it really doesn't make any difference to me. I don't need his approval." She headed back to the bedroom, keeping her head turned away to hide the moisture that threatened to spill from her eyes. No sense making a big deal out of it, and Ginger surely would if she thought her feelings were hurt.

Back in the privacy of the bedroom, Marta took off the dress, but not before she took another long look in the mirror. There was nothing wrong with the way she looked. Nothing. She finished changing and pasted a smile on her face. The best thing to do was act like she always did. It would be easy. She'd had years of experience hiding her feelings.

Marta found Ginger in the kitchen. "I thought I'd make some popcorn and we could watch a movie. What do you say, Ginger? Does that sound like a good idea?"

One thing Marta admired about Ginger was her ability to swiftly change her mood to an upbeat one. It didn't matter whether she was mad or crying. Five minutes later she would be smiling and looking at the bright side of things. Soon they were seated side by side on the old sofa, sharing a bowl of buttered popcorn and watching a sappy love story on TV. The only problem was, the hero looked just like Josh. Every time he appeared on the screen, it reminded Marta of the expression on Josh's face when he'd walked out the front door. She finally found if she looked at the wall where the paint was peeling, instead of at the Josh look-alike, the resemblance didn't bother her as much.

"Oh isn't that so romantic?" Ginger apparently hadn't noticed the likeness between her brother and the guy on TV. She was sniffling into her paper towel which Marta had given her to wipe the butter off her fingers. "Don't you love it when he looks at her like that?"

"Oh, man, Ginger. It isn't real, you know. This is just a fairy tale, made into a movie so they can sell more panty hose and baby food. Haven't you ever wondered why all the commercials are geared toward women? They know there isn't a man alive who buys into this stuff."

"Are you still mad at Josh?"

Marta rolled her eyes. What did Josh have to do with anything? Thank goodness the movie was nearly over. She was ready to call it a night. The movie was boring and unrealistic, but she sat through it to please Ginger.

Just as the predictable ending violin music rose in volume, the door opened and Josh came in. Marta deliberately avoided looking at his face. The last thing she wanted to see before going to bed was the censure she'd witnessed earlier.

"Hi." He walked over and stood in front of her. She had no choice. It was look at the wall, or look into his eyes. Did he have to stand so close? His nearness was making her feel a little . . . itchy.

Ginger jumped up from the sofa. "I'm gonna take a shower. See you two in the morning."

Marta started to rise, too, but Josh sat in Ginger's vacated spot. "I'd like to talk to you."

77

"About what?" Yes, she was definitely feeling uncomfortable. Were her eyes beginning to water again? She would not to cry.

"I acted like a jerk. Would you please forgive me?"

She had to get away from him. Her face felt hot and her nose was starting to run. "There's nothing to forgive."

"I think there is. When I saw you all gussied up like that, I got worried you'd leave. I was kinda getting used to having you around and you took me by surprise, that's all."

Marta took several short breaths. "Ok, I forgive you. If that's all, I'd like to go to bed." She took several more rapid breaths and leaned forward to stand.

"Not quite all. I brought you a peace offering. A present to show you I'm sorry. It's something you said you wanted the very first day you arrived here." Josh reached inside his coat and pulled out a tiny gray bundle of fur.

"A cat! Get that thing out of here! Get it away from me!" Marta leaped from the sofa and ran from the room wheezing.

CHAPTER SEVEN

"How was I supposed to know she's allergic to cats?" Josh ran his hands through his hair and glared at Ginger. "I distinctly remember you saying Marta wanted a kitten."

"Umm, I don't remember saying that, Josh. Truly I don't. You must have misunderstood."

Josh blew out a rapid breath. He knew very well he hadn't misunderstood. Ginger wasn't telling the truth. He hated deception. And in this case there was absolutely no justification for it. Inflicting misery on another human being galled him. Worse yet, Marta was still in bed, suffering from his well-intentioned, but poisonous gift.

"I don't believe you for one minute, Ginger." He bent down and flipped open the lid of the vacuum cleaner so he could take out the bag in case it contained any offending cat hairs. "I'm hauling this outside, but I'll be right back and you had better have your explanation, a *truthful* explanation, ready."

When Josh returned from the dumpster, his sister was nowhere in sight. He could hear low voices and an occasional sneeze coming from the gals' bedroom. Before he confronted anyone, he'd better remove his clothes and stick them in the washing machine. They were probably covered with cat hairs too. He looked down as he unbuttoned his shirt and noticed the scratches on his hands. That poor little fur ball had nearly jumped out of its skin when Marta shrieked and ran. It was safe now . . . back with its original owners. Needless to say, they hadn't been overjoyed about taking the kitten back.

Josh stepped out of jeans and slammed them into the machine with his shirt and jacket. He opened the dryer and grabbed a bath towel to wrap around his waist. He could just imagine the howling that would follow if either Marta or Ginger caught him parading around the apartment in his underwear. Those two were always casting him as the bad guy. And all he'd done was try to be nice. He'd even overlooked his own rule against pets in order to please Marta. And what did he get? Yelled at for allegedly trying to kill her, that's what.

He glanced at the kitchen clock. It was after midnight. He should be in bed by now. By the time he had his shower, and got to sleep it would be close to one.

Several hours later Josh lay in bed tapping his fingers on the blanket. The neon green numbers on the digital clock showed two o'clock. The later it got, the more awake he felt. He rolled over onto his back. If he could find a comfortable position, maybe he could go to sleep. Marta was never going to stay now. And why should she? They were all cramped in this small apartment. She didn't even have her own room. He'd been stupid to think all he had to do was bring her gifts. It would be just his luck if she was allergic to copper pots too.

It was silly for him to go to all this effort. He'd eaten TV dinners before she arrived and he could get used to them again. He squeezed his eyes shut and Marta's face appeared, the way it had looked earlier in the evening, standing before him in one of her new outfits. She'd been so beautiful. Her hair, her mouth, the way the dress fit her. He hadn't known what to say. He didn't have the words to tell her what he really thought. That's when he realized she was way out of his league. She belonged somewhere else. Not here, in this ratty apartment building, taking care of his needs.

He'd felt like a jerk when he realized he'd hurt her feelings. Instead of swallowing his pride and apologizing right then, he'd taken the easy way out. If anyone had told him a year ago he'd be losing sleep over a woman, he would have thought they were nuts. Now it was him that was nuts. "Ahhh, nuts!" He punched his pillow and rolled back over onto his side.

***

Marta took a seat across the desk from a man who didn't look much older than herself. He flicked her application toward her with an air of dismissal. There was no mistaking what that meant. He wasn't even going to say, "We'll call you." This was the third interview that day. Each more depressing than the last. Even the rain outside added to her misery.

"I'd be willing to go to night school to get some computer training. I'm a fast learner."

The man in front of her looked as if he was actually enjoying her discomfort. He leaned back in his leather chair, laced his hands behind his head and put both feet up on his desk. "Frankly, Miss, P- uh, Miss, there are quite a few people we're interviewing for this position. Most of them have college degrees."

"For a receptionist position? You're looking for someone with a college degree?" Marta wondered how much training this guy thought it took to answer the phone, smile, and say, "Hello, someone will be with you in a moment."

"This isn't just any position." The man paused and glanced at her application with distaste. "It's one of the most prestigious accounting firms in the northwest. Our clients have certain expectations of our staff, so we have high standards, right down to the lowliest receptionist."

Marta looked at the man in amazement. What arrogance! Why had she bothered dressing nicely to apply for a job which evidently was the lowliest of lows in company hierarchy? He treated her as if she were a fraud because she didn't have a degree. What would his reaction have been if she had told him where and how she grew up? Call security and have her escorted to the door? She rose, retrieved her application and left without thanking him.

Her bus arrived early, making her run to catch it. She'd forgotten to bring an umbrella, so by the time she paid her fare and found a seat, her face and hair were a wet mess from the freezing rain. She didn't care. Nobody on this bus cared, that's for sure. They were wet too, and most of them looked as tired as her. The woman seated next to her held a lunch bag on her lap. She must be going home from work. Her clothes and make-up were fashionable and perfect for a professional woman. A pang of envy knifed through Marta's chest. When were circumstances going to change for her?

"Hi. I'm Ivy. I haven't seen you on this bus before. Where do you work?"

After the day she'd had, the woman's question depressed her. Should she tell her the truth? That she couldn't find a job? She couldn't bear to see the pity in the other woman's eyes.

"Well, actually, I don't work downtown. I was shopping at Nordstrom's and when I got ready to leave, I discovered my car had been stolen." Marta took a deep breath. "I don't usually ride the bus," she emphasized.

"Oh, dear! That must have been awful for you. I hope you have insurance."

"Oh yes. My er, husband insists on insurance, the car being so valuable and all."

"That's good. What kind of car is it?"

Marta didn't know anything about cars. Why had she ever started telling these stupid lies? To a woman she'd never seen before and would never see again? Did the opinion of a complete stranger matter so much to her? Sure, it was fun to wear beautiful clothes and pretend she was *Somebody*. But where would the deception stop? Was her entire future going to be based on a pattern of falsehoods?

"Oh! Here's my stop." Marta stood and signaled the driver. "It was delightful meeting you." She hurried to the rear door and stepped off the bus the minute it opened. Her hands were shaking. Exhaust fumes stung her eyes. She looked around and realized she didn't know where she was and began to walk toward the retreating bus.

"Next time I'll bring my umbrella," she muttered. The rain turned to sleet that pricked her cheeks. She had to keep her head down because she was walking directly into the wind. Puddles of water formed on the sidewalk, and the adjoining gutter flowed like a small river. Marta quickly looked up to see if she could spot any familiar landmarks. She couldn't see anything further away than a few blocks. What she could see made her uneasy. She was evidently in the industrial area south of the city's business center.

Marta kept trudging along, praying another bus would come by. Darkness would fall soon. Even when she'd lived on the streets as a teenager, she'd never felt this apprehensive. At least she'd always been with other people in those days. Now she was alone. She couldn't see a soul anywhere. The buildings didn't even have windows, or if they did they were boarded up. If she only had enough money for a taxi, she'd hail one. It wouldn't have mattered, though. There weren't any taxis cruising around this area. There wasn't anything. Except maybe rats. Hadn't she heard there were rats all over the area near the waterfront? Big ones. How close was she to the docks?

Marta walked faster, no longer caring if she stepped in puddles. The discomfort of wet feet paled in comparison to the horrible fanged things that might jump out at her from every alleyway she passed. She should have stayed on the bus. She'd be almost home by now. Ginger and Josh would begin worrying about her soon. Josh. Oh how she wished his truck would appear now. The only problem was, it wasn't going to happen. Even if by some miracle he did come looking for her, he'd never think to look for her here.

A parking lot! Marta raced toward the rows of cars ahead. Where there were cars, there had to be people. And a telephone. Cold water splashed on her legs as she ran. Her wet pantyhose stuck to her skin, making each stride an effort. She didn't care. There were lights up ahead. She hurried even faster, anxious to escape the darkness that pursued her.

"Josh. Oh please be home," Marta whispered as she fumbled to put the right change into the phone. Now that she was standing still, she realized how cold it was. She tried to wiggle her toes, positive they had turned to ice cubes. The phone booth offered little protection from the wind. She held the receiver to her ear with her right hand, but kept her left hand in the pocket of her coat.

"Hello."

"Oh, Josh. Thank God. You can't believe the day I've had. Please come get me."

"Marta! Is that you? Are you crying? Where are you?"

"I'm not crying. I'm only sniffing from the cold. But I need you." She gave him the address where he could find her.

***

Josh drove as fast as the speed limit would allow, maybe faster. What was Marta doing in that part of the city, anyway? Didn't she know there were places that weren't safe for a woman after dark? Surely she wasn't looking for a job there! He braked hard at a red light, narrowly stopping in time. He'd given her a raise and treated her as well, even better than most bosses. Why wasn't she satisfied with what she had?

After what seemed like forever, the light turned green and he guided his truck through the dark streets, keeping an eye out for the address Marta had given him. Some of the buildings looked as if they were about to fall down. Graffiti covered the walls in places. Josh didn't even want to imagine what some of the graphics signified. A bum sat in a doorway, drinking from a paper bag. Thank God Marta hadn't stumbled into *him*. He might have mugged her or worse.

At last, the parking lot she'd described came into view. He scanned the area looking for a phone booth. The one where he'd told her to wait. Only one phone booth was visible. The door was missing and no one was inside. A quick look around the area netted nothing. No Marta. Not even a parking lot attendant. Josh could feel his heartbeat quicken and he took a deep breath. He had to keep a cool head.

The lot appeared to be for employee parking for a nearby warehouse. Perhaps she had gone inside to wait where it was warm and dry. He drove up and down a few rows of parked vehicles, hoping to catch a glimpse of her in his headlights. Nothing. No visitor parking spaces available near the door either, but he didn't care. He parked right in front of the entrance and stepped out. The lettering on the door had faded so long ago, the name of the business had totally disappeared. Josh reached out a hand, turned the door handle, and shoved. The door refused to budge.

Josh pounded on the door with his fist. What kind of business kept its door locked, anyway? After waiting all of thirty seconds and getting a lack of response from his knock, he swung his foot back and gave the door a kick. He'd take the door off its hinges if necessary. Was someone inside keeping her prisoner? Why else would the door be locked? If anybody harmed a hair on her head, he'd rip them apart. He lifted his foot again.

"Josh!"

He swung around. The most beautiful sight in the world was running toward him. "Marta!" He took a step toward her and she crashed into his arms. "Thank God, you're ok! Where were you?" He pulled her into his chest, holding her tightly, her drenched hair solidly against his cheek. "You're ok." He could feel her trembling so he squeezed her harder.

"I waited in the phone booth, but before you got here, a man drove past two or three times." Her voice was muffled against his coat.

Josh thrust her slightly away and looked into her face.

"Did he hurt you? If he did, I'll ki-"

"No. He didn't hurt me, but he made me nervous so I hid in an unlocked car after he drove out of sight."

"Let's get you home. You're shivering." He guided her to his truck and helped her inside. Once in the driver's seat, he started the engine and turned the heater on full blast. The fan pushed warm air around the cab, but Josh feared they'd be home before it got really warm inside. Before putting the truck in gear, he shrugged out of his jacket. "Here, wrap this around you."

"Thanks."

"You're welcome." He turned his attention to getting out of the parking lot and headed toward home. Marta would need a hot bath in order to thoroughly warm up. Once she was home, warm and dry, he'd give her a lecture on safety. If she hadn't cared enough about herself to keep away from such isolated areas, she should at least consider whether she was worrying her roommates to death. This was the irresponsible kind of thing Ginger might do. He would never have expected it from Marta. How was he supposed to keep her safe when she didn't use common sense?

"I'm really sorry, Josh."

"We'll talk about it later."

"I need to talk about it now. I don't want you to think I make a habit of getting lost or expecting you, or anyone for that matter, to come to my rescue."

"You were lost? I would have thought even a child couldn't have gotten *that* lost."

"You have good reason to be upset. But I didn't end up there on purpose."

Josh turned the wheel and accelerated the truck up the freeway on-ramp. "If you don't mind explaining, how exactly did you come to be a mile away from downtown Seattle? Isn't that where you said you were headed this morning?"

"Uh, I kinda got off at the wrong bus stop. I *was* on my way home, you know."

Josh hit the top of the steering wheel with the palm of his hand. "That's about the lamest story I've ever heard. That's right up there with some teenager telling her parents, *'Sorry, we ran out of gas.'*"

"I don't care if you believe me or not. That's what happened. It won't happen again, but if it does, I won't bother calling you."

"You're right. It won't happen again because you're not going off by yourself anymore." Josh wondered if Marta even had a clue about how much she had scared him.

"Excuse me? You're telling me where I can and can't go? I'm not your sister and you have no right to make those decisions for me."

"Well, somebody has to. You don't seem capable of taking care of yourself." Josh regretted those words as soon as he'd spoken them. This was escalating into a fight. He glanced over at her and could tell he'd made her angry by the stubborn jut of her chin.

"I'm sorry, Marta. I didn't mean that the way it sounded."

"Oh, you meant it. Look at the way you boss your sister around. You treat her like a little kid. You smother her."

Josh took a deep breath. This conversation was definitely getting out of hand. "I don't hear Ginny complaining."

"Of course not. She loves you and wants to please you."

"And you could care less whether you please me or not." The realization made Josh's stomach knot up. Of course, Marta's opinion didn't matter to him. But that was a lie. It mattered to him a great deal. The freeway exit leading home came into view and relief coursed through him. He'd heard enough. Said enough.

***

Marta leaned back in the tub and prayed her body temperature would quickly rise from sub-freezing. Even the blast of heat from the truck's dashboard hadn't cut the chill of Josh's silence the last few blocks home. So he thought she was a total idiot. What else was new? He really would have had reason to think that, if she'd told him the whole story. Then he hadn't made her feel any better when he insinuated she didn't care what he thought about her. Of course she did. She'd have told him the truth if she didn't care. After all, he was her best friend's brother.

At least she'd gotten her point across. She didn't think he'd try and restrict her activities after she'd pointed out he didn't own her. Marta sank lower in the tub. Her skin tingled from the hot water, but her bones still felt cold. She stuck one foot out of the water and turned the hot water faucet with her toes. A trickle of steaming water kept the chill off as she forced her muscles to relax and closed her eyes.

It was too late to change Josh's opinion of her. Josh was probably telling Ginger right now that Marta was too dumb to live. It wouldn't be the first time someone had said it, but she'd learned to live with it. *"Hey Martha! Where's your mom and Dad? Mr. and Mrs. Thompson aren't your real parents. You're just a welfare kid. You were too ugly and stupid for your own folks to keep you."* How many times had she heard those very words? Plenty, but they didn't have the power to cut her anymore.

Marta wiped a tear from her cheeks, stood and reached for a towel.

CHAPTER EIGHT

Marta spent the next few days avoiding Josh. She continued to work hard at the apartment house, but managed to spend two more afternoons meeting with prospective employers. Josh hadn't said any more about the night he'd come and picked her up. However she could plainly see the disapproval in his eyes each time she left with her "interview" clothes on.

Miss Treymore had proven to be a valuable friend and gave her some pointers on how to conduct herself during an interview. She'd even dug around in her closet and come up with an attaché case for Marta to use to carry her credentials and resume in. The first item she put into it was a glowing letter of recommendation which Mona's husband had given her. A trip to the library netted her some time on a computer to type a resume. She was even able to go through a word-processing tutorial while she was there.

Marta gained confidence with each interview. As a result, two office managers had called her to come back for a second interview. Neither job appealed to her, but she couldn't afford to be choosy. They paid a little better than she was getting working for Josh. And . . . they would be a step toward her goal of getting out and meeting people. Rather, meeting a particular kind of man, who would be her ticket into a circle of the right kind of people.

Ginger repeatedly cautioned her about setting unrealistic sights, but Marta knew she had it in her to succeed. In fact, already a very good-looking business man she'd met at a downtown office had asked her out. He'd even been rather persistent. It was only after she'd pointedly stared at his wedding band, that he'd backed down. Some people might criticize her goals, but they'd never be able to find fault with her morals. Married men were off limits. Period.

Other than that, she wasn't going to be picky. Her dates didn't need to be handsome. In fact, it wouldn't hurt if they were a little on the homely side. They'd be less likely to stray. If she found one who met all her criteria and they wanted to marry her, she would make it her priority to be a good wife. She'd even insist on a prenuptial agreement. After all, she wasn't planning to bleed someone dry and then run. A good marriage took work, commitment and was for life.

"There's a UPS truck here." Ginger called out from the living room. "Are you expecting another shipment from Portland?"

Marta laughed. Mona's husband had already sent her enough things to open her own boutique. "Nope, it must be something Josh ordered." She walked to the window and stood next to Ginger. Sure enough, Josh came trotting around the building and took a huge box from the driver.

"We have no shame, peeking out the window like a couple of kids at Christmas. Josh will accuse us of having nothing better to do and give us both chores." Ginger giggled and bounced to the door to let Josh in.

"That must not be more plumbing supplies or you would have taken that to the shed."

Josh set the box on the floor and grinned at both women. "Nope, it's not plumbing supplies. It's a present." He searched Marta's face as if to gauge her reaction. "For the apartment."

Ginger looked closely at the writing on the box. "Why Josh. This is from that TV shopping program. Did you buy us a ton of gold jewelry? Hurry. Open it up!"

Josh pulled a pocket knife from his pants pocket. "Nope. It's not gold, but you're getting close. Think of another precious mineral."

"Diamonds! You did buy us jewelry! And it's weeks and weeks till Christmas. Hurry and get that lid off. We want to see."

Marta observed Josh cut the tape on the box. He glanced at her again, but she quickly looked away. She still smarted from the argument they'd had the night in his truck. She should leave the room. However, Ginger and Josh's enthusiasm was contagious. Keeping her distance, she stayed and watched. Josh squatted on his heels and pulled some packing paper out. He carefully folded it and set it aside.

"Hurry up, Josh."

Josh's laugh boomed out and his eyes crinkled in amusement. "If I tell you it isn't diamonds, will you stop jumping from one foot to another?" He pulled another piece of paper out and folded it slower and more carefully than before. "Take a cue from Marta. See how patiently she stands way over there."

Marta didn't want to be used as an example. Especially by someone who really didn't think she had any good qualities and merely humored her. Why did he think she stood on the opposite side of the room? "It's because I don't particularly care what's in the box." She slapped her hand over her mouth. Had she really blurted that lie out loud? It sounded so mean. Luckily it must have gone right over their heads. They didn't even look up from their unpacking. Ginger had dropped to her knees and was digging in the box too.

"Here it comes." They each took a side and tugged. "Oh, look, Marta!" She held up a huge copper baking pan. Josh pulled out a matching lid. Soon a half dozen different sized pans dotted the floor like giant shiny pennies. Her two roommates looked at her expectantly. Was she supposed to say something?

"Uh. Nice pans."

Ginger stood and excitedly thrust a large pot toward her. "Is that all? Nice pans? Think of all the things you can cook in these."

"These are for me to cook in? They look rather expensive."

Josh spoke up. "Not too expensive when you consider their quality. They're made to last a lifetime."

Marta didn't need to be bonked in the head with a plank. Since she was the only one around who actually cooked, or actually cared about getting a wholesome meal on the table, the pans must be for her. A not-so-subtle hint from Josh who thought she should spend her life in somebody's kitchen. Where she could be watched. And controlled. The array of copper pots must have cost him a fortune. More than the salary she could earn, working for him in a month. Should she tell him his attempted manipulation had failed, or let him figure it out for himself?

"I'm sorry. But words just fail me." She didn't care if her sarcasm showed or not. She'd cook their meals in his shiny pots, but each day brought her closer to the time she wouldn't be anyone's household help. Now she knew why he didn't have a steady girlfriend. As soon as he whipped out his checkbook and bought them a bright yellow pair of rubber galoshes, like the ones she'd found outside her door one morning, they probably headed for the hills, laughing their heads off. He'd be left holding the boots and wondering why the local florists hadn't added such swell things to their inventories.

Not that Josh should have brought her flowers or anything like that. It's just that he always expected her to get excited about the dumbest things. The pots were nice. There. She admitted it. But the thought behind them was not nice. Bribery, pure and simple. She turned from the room. "I think I'll go out for a little walk."

***

"I guess she doesn't like copper pots." Josh looked at his sister, hoping she could shed some light on Marta's strange behavior.

"I think your gift just overwhelmed her, Josh."

"Don't try to spare my feelings or gloss things over, Ginger. It's more than the pots. She's upset about something. In fact she seemed upset about more than these things for the kitchen."

"If you must know, Josh, I don't think she plans on staying with us much longer. She probably sees the pots as a way of trying to tie her here."

"I know she's been looking for a job. But you think she's planning on moving right away too? Why?" Josh didn't like the sound of this. He didn't much like any kind of change. Things were running smoothly. Why did Marta have to ruin things? Couldn't she see he was trying to make things comfortable for her? Didn't she know how badly he and Ginger wanted her to stay? He'd knocked himself out trying to show her.

"Josh, I can see you've finally come to accept her, but I think it's time we both faced the facts. Marta is . . . well, Marta is kinda warped."

"For crying out loud, Ginger! She's your best friend. How could you say something like that about her?" Was his sister losing her mind? Or was he losing his? Marta was fine. In fact, one of the most fine women he'd ever met.

"You don't have to yell at me." Ginger sniffed loudly, her usual warning of impending tears.

"I didn't yell." He took a step toward her. "But you'd better explain."

Ginger snuffled some more, glancing at Josh to gauge the effect. He tapped his foot impatiently. Her tricks could only work so many times. He wasn't going to let her off the hook.

"I'm waiting."

"Well. You know how hard it was for us growing up."

Josh gazed at the ceiling. Was this going to be one of Ginger's long stories?

"Marta always hated the way we lived back then. She vowed she would never be poor when she grew up."

"So who says she's poor? She's got a job. A roof over her head and plenty to eat. Not to mention a closet full of clothes that Princess Diana would have envied. Make that *several* closets full of clothes."

"She wants more. She wants to be rich." Ginger mumbled the last couple of words, but Josh heard.

"And this is why she's looking for jobs downtown? It's so important to her to make a lot of money?"

"It's everything to her, Josh. I just thought you should know. I can tell you're starting to really care for her. I don't want you to be disappointed."

"That's it? You're telling me everything?"

"Uh, that's all I know for sure. Please don't tell her I said anything to you, Josh. She's kind of a private person."

Josh ran his fingers through his hair. Private person? Or was secretive a better word? She'd never shared any of this with him. Didn't she think he'd understand? Had she forgotten he'd grown up in the same situation? He walked to the window and looked out. He'd reacted to his childhood in a similar way. He was thirty years old and had been breaking his butt since he was a teenager, just to make something of himself. How could he possibly judge Marta for doing the same thing?

He turned to ask Ginger's opinion about how they . . . how he could help Marta, but she'd slipped out of the room. No wonder Marta was unhappy. She'd viewed his actions as an obstruction to her plans. He wouldn't deny his motives had been selfish. He wanted her to stay. He wanted to see her every morning at breakfast, all during the day and at dinner. He'd even hoped for more. Wanted her snuggled against him every night. For the rest of their lives. That was his fantasy, though. It was never hers.

He kicked the empty box. What a joke. He'd sat on Miss Treymore's couch and believed everything the TV saleswoman had said about copper pots making any woman deliriously happy. Every last signal Marta had given him about her intentions had gone right over his head. No, that was wrong. He'd seen and heard plenty, he just hadn't wanted to believe she'd actually leave. Even when she was dressed up, looking like some classy society dame, he'd fooled himself into thinking he had a chance with her someday. Someday when he could afford a wife. The truth was, he never had a chance. She was way out of his class. And if Ginger were right, Marta knew it as well as he did.

Josh carried the pots and pans into the kitchen. He refused to consider returning them. If Marta could enjoy them for a week or a month, that was fine. He didn't care what she served him for meals or how she cooked it. It was all going to taste like cardboard. He busied himself nailing hooks on the wall for hanging the pots. They'd be visible every day to remind him of what a fool he'd been.

He narrowly missed smashing himself with the hammer. Barely nicking the corner of his thumbnail, he stuck it in his mouth. At least no one was around to witness his frustration. His thumb stopped throbbing and he nailed the far end of the utensil rack to the wall. He hung the assortment of slotted spoons, a wire whisk, and some other gadgets whose purpose he couldn't fathom. It all looked good hanging there. The copper pots made the kitchen look homey. The TV display had included green plants scattered around, but they didn't come with the set. Maybe he'd get some the next time he was at the nursery.

Josh heard the front door open and assumed his roommates had returned. Only one set of footsteps moved toward the kitchen, however. It was Marta. His heart jumped when he saw her. Even with her hair mussed up from the wind and rain, she looked beautiful.

"Ginny's not with you?"

"No. I haven't seen her since I left. Did you look in the bedroom?"

Josh saw Marta's gaze shift over to the hanging utensils. He read approval in her eyes but her expression quickly changed to neutral when she realized he was watching her. Now that he understood the significance of what he'd done, he spoke quickly, to get her mind on something else. "Oh. She left shortly after you did. She's probably visiting friends."

"I don't believe I've met any of her friends. Does she have lots?"

"Quite a few. None are what I'd call close friends. She has a large circle of acquaintances she does things with."

"What does she do? When she goes out, that is."

"She goes to dances and movies. In the summer she likes those rock and roll concerts in the park, or on the Seattle Center grounds. Once or twice a month she volunteers a weekend at the women's shelter."

Marta looked as if she were mulling over his words and frowned. "I've been here nearly a month and she's never gone anywhere." A touch of regret colored her statement.

Josh smiled at her. "You can bet Ginger would have gone and dragged you along, if she really wanted to go. I think she had so much fun catching up with you, she just didn't notice the weeks go by." He tried to read Marta's thoughts, but she remained as much a mystery to him as the day he met her. She looked from him to the pots and back again.

"I hope she's having a good time tonight, then. She deserves to have fun."

"And she'll tell us all about it when she gets home, complete with hand gestures and repeating any jokes she's heard. Let's have a cup of coffee while we wait." Josh reached for the pot and filled it with water. Aware of the lingering tension between them, he tried to act as nonchalant as possible.

***

Marta sat on the sofa with her cup of steaming coffee and watched Josh kick back in his recliner. She'd been on guard when she returned, afraid he'd bring up those dratted pots again. But he hadn't. In fact he seemed to be trying to put her at ease. She tipped the cup to her mouth and blew across the surface of the fragrant brew. Hazelnut. One of her favorite flavors.

Josh reached for the remote control. "Anything you'd like to see on TV tonight?"

"No. I don't think I'll stay up very long. Just until Ginger gets home." She curled her legs under her. She wondered what Ginger and Josh had eaten for dinner. This evening was the first time they hadn't eaten together since she'd been living with them. She felt a little guilty for taking off like she had, and hoped they hadn't gone without supper because of her.

Josh turned the TV on and she expected him to turn the channel to view a football game.

"Look. Here's something you'll enjoy."

Marta turned her eyes toward the small TV screen and saw a pair of beautifully costumed figure skaters gliding over the ice. They moved in unison and if she squinted, it could have been one skater instead of two. She loved that kind of harmony. A harmony that had been lacking in her relationship with her roommates. When people were out of step with each other, it doomed them to failure. If she had been honest with Josh from the beginning about her plans, he wouldn't have held onto his expectations of her. Now she was afraid their budding friendship was in jeopardy.

Josh glanced away from the screen and smiled at her. Was he pretending to enjoy the program for her benefit? He was a decent man . . . too nice to deceive. She would tell him the truth. It was better to risk his censure than to have these constant misunderstandings. If he judged her harshly for being shallow and mercenary, so be it. At least she wouldn't have the burden of keeping secrets anymore.

Marta took another sip of her coffee. How should she start? Could she explain her plans to Josh in such a way that wouldn't make her seem to be a money grubbing gold digger? Most people would think that. Especially people like Josh, who worked hard for a living. Would he understand that no matter how hard she worked, she would never really amount to anything? Marta sighed. Probably not. He sat there so relaxed and comfortable with himself. A strong, but simple man. The kind you could count on. The kind of man most women would jump at the chance to marry. He was even handsome when he smiled. He smiled a lot.

The harsh ring of the phone interrupted her thoughts. She took in the way the soft flannel fabric of Josh's shirt stretched tautly over his wide chest as he reached for the receiver. Most men spent a lot of money and hours in the gym developing a body like his. Josh's build came naturally, from the hard work he did around the apartments. She couldn't quite picture Josh at a gym. He wasn't vain enough to spend hours exercising for the sole purpose of looking good.

"Hello."

Marta knew from experience Josh's deep voice sounded sexy over the phone. Especially when he put feeling into his words . . . like now. What was he saying? His face turned pale. Marta reached over and grabbed the remote to lower the volume on the TV.

"Are you sure it's Ginger? My sister?" The concern in his voice rapidly changed to alarm. "We'll be right there."

"What is it, Josh?" Marta stood at the same time as he did, suddenly frightened at the panic twisting his features.

"That was the hospital just outside the city. Ginger's been in some kind of accident. They want me to come right away." He bent and picked up Marta's shoes, thrusting them toward her. "Come on. I need you with me."

Marta hopped from foot to foot, putting her shoes on while following him as he raced out the door. An accident? Ginny? How bad was it? One look at Josh's face as they pulled out of the parking lot, told her it was bad enough. She squeezed her eyes shut as they squealed around a corner, and prayed Ginny would be OK. Oh, God. She had to be OK. Ginny was the only family Marta had.

Marta continued to pray while she chewed on her lower lip as the street lights whizzed by. She wanted to ask Josh for more information but didn't want to break his intense concentration on the traffic. Her grip tightened on the armrest. How far was it to the hospital? It seemed like it was taking forever to get there. Josh continued speeding along, until they began climbing a hill. Soon the large hospital building loomed ahead of them. Josh expertly swung the pickup into a parking space near the emergency entrance.

"Well, at least we're lucky she's here. This hospital has one of the finest trauma centers in the area."

"Trauma?" Marta blanched. This sounded worse and worse. She ran to keep up with Josh as he sprinted toward the lighted doors ahead.

The automatic doors barely opened in time for Josh and Marta to speed through. Inside, mass of confusion reigned, at least in her eyes. People of all ages filled the chairs in a waiting area. Several people behind a counter were handing out forms to those who hadn't found a seat yet. Marta looked around for someone who could direct them to Ginger, but everywhere she looked, a line of people loomed ahead of them.

Suddenly Josh grabbed her wrist and whipped her along with him toward a set of double doors. A sign plainly warned them not to go beyond that point since they weren't hospital personnel, but she was powerless to slow Josh down.

"Hold it!" A man in a uniform stepped in front of them just as they'd made it through the doors. "You can't come in here."

"I've got to see my sister." Josh attempted to go around the man who stepped in front of them and held up his hand.

"You can't come in here. Now if you'll just have a seat outside, I'll send someone out to talk to you. What is your sister's name?"

Marta felt Josh's tense beside her. She instinctively knew he was debating whether to flatten the man who was holding them back. Josh calmed himself enough to tell him Ginger's full name so she sighed in relief. Had the security guard used force or been less kind, Marta had no doubt Josh would've done something foolish. She smiled gratefully at the man who no doubt was used to dealing with distressed people.

Marta stayed close to Josh as they returned to the waiting area and wedged themselves onto a bench next to a man who smelled like a winery. A winery in a dumpster. Marta wrinkled her nose in distaste. However, there were no other empty places to sit in the entire room. Every seat was full and people who hadn't found a seat leaned against the walls. The noise was deafening. A young mother tried to shush a crying baby who tugged at his ear. A woman seated on the other side of Josh let out a moan every few moments. A TV mounted on brackets against a far wall blared away but as far as Marta could tell, nobody paid any attention to it.

Marta leaned toward Josh and he took her hand, nearly crushing it in his grip. She could see the fear in his eyes, but the set of his jaw told her he had strength enough to face whatever was ahead. The eerie wail of a siren drew closer and Marta glimpsed an ambulance pulling up outside the building. She hated hospitals. The sounds, the smells, and everything they represented. She'd never viewed them as a place of help . . . only a place of death.

Josh's fingers tightened against hers each time someone from the hospital staff called another name. It seemed as if every eye in the room was fixed on the entrance to the waiting area. Half hoping for news of a loved one, and the other half impatiently waiting their turn with a doctor. Marta lightly stroked Josh's arm with her free hand. This had to be harder for him than her. A man like Josh needed to be in control. Not helplessly waiting.

"It's going to be OK, Josh." Marta spoke the words as if saying them would make it so. Josh's eyes turned toward her and she noticed their color had deepened to a dark blue.

"Ginger Morton family?" A woman in green surgical scrubs stood in the doorway, holding a bundle of clothes.

"That's us." Josh started to rise, but the woman gestured for him to stay seated.

"Miss Morton has been taken to surgery and will be there for a while. A doctor will be out to speak with you later. Here are her things." She thrust the bundle toward Josh and Marta.

Before Josh or Marta had a chance to ask any questions, the woman disappeared, leaving the wrinkled, soiled, clothing in Marta's arms. She looked down at them. They could have at least put them in a bag, she thought to herself. She recognized the things Ginger had worn when they'd all been together earlier in the evening. It seemed like light years ago. Now they were wrinkled and covered in a sticky red substance. Marta tried to fold the clothes before Josh saw, but it was too late.

"Is-is that . . . what I think?" Josh's eyes were trained on the stained pile of clothing on Marta's lap. His complexion matched the pallor of the greenish white wall behind him and sweat beaded on his forehead.

Marta ran her index finger through the damp crimson substance on Ginger's jeans. "It's not what you think, Josh." She held her finger up to his face for him to see but he didn't respond. Instead the last bit of color drained from his face just before he slumped over and landed face down in her lap.

CHAPTER NINE

"Josh!" Marta hung onto him in an attempt to keep him from sliding to the floor. "Josh, can you hear me? It's OK. Ginger's NOT dead!" She tried to shake him and hold on to him at the same time. "She's not dead."

"Oh, honey. Denial is natural when a loved one dies. You just have to accept it."

Marta glared at the woman seated next to Josh who had just given this piece of helpful information. "She's NOT dead! Nobody's dead. Didn't you hear me? Josh, can you hear me? Wake up."

"It's just the shock. He'll come out of it. Then you'll both have to learn to grieve." The woman's strident voice pushed on, making Marta want to smack her.

"There's NOTHING to grieve over. Please, will you just be quiet?" Marta shook Josh again, aware all eyes in the room were now on her.

"Ya want me to throw some water on him?" The drunk seated next to Marta had apparently roused himself due to the commotion.

"No!" Marta hugged Josh tighter as if to protect him from all the derelicts of the city. "Would everybody please just leave us alone?" Marta strained to lift Josh into an upright position. He was going to be so embarrassed to find he'd actually fainted. And at the sight of tomato sauce.

Josh moaned and shook his head. Another ambulance pulled up outside and everyone's attention shifted to the new occupants of the waiting room from hell. At least everyone there was a stranger and they wouldn't likely meet any of them again. No telling what Josh would do when he discovered he'd compromised his masculine dignity by passing out. Marta discreetly kicked Ginger's clothes under her chair. No use taking a chance Josh would see them and repeat his nosedive into her lap. Next time he might hit the floor and then she'd have two people to visit in the hospital.

***

"Feeling better?"

"What happened?" Josh rubbed his temple with the tips of his fingers. It didn't ease the throbbing pain.

"Uh, I think you must have dozed off for a little while."

Josh stared into her warm brown eyes. It was coming back to him. And he wanted to kiss her for not dwelling on it. "Is she . . . any word?"

Marta smiled at him. "No. But I was just about to go ask at the desk. Stay here, I'll be right back."

"I'll go."

"No. Let me." She leaned toward him and whispered, "I need to get away from that creep sitting next to me for a while."

Josh watched Marta gracefully wind her way through the rows of people and chairs. He ran his fingers through his hair. What was the matter with him anyway? His little sister was probably dying on a surgeon's table somewhere in the hospital and here he was ogling her best friend. Was he doomed to always have Marta on his mind? He'd better get over it. Her future life wasn't going to include him. He tapped his foot impatiently.

"Did your wife go to find a priest?"

Josh swung his head around to face the woman in the chair next to his. "We don't need a priest. And she's not my wife."

"Humph! You coulda fooled me. But then you young people don't have any respect for marriage these days, living together the way you do. I s'pose the last rites mean nothing to ya either. Take my advice, sonny. You need a priest."

Josh stiffened his spine. "If anyone is going to need the last rites, it's going-"

"Josh." Marta had returned and tugged his sleeve. "We're in the wrong waiting room. We're supposed to be on third floor in the surgical waiting room." She pulled him to his feet.

Two people plopped into the vacated chairs almost before Josh stepped away from them.

The man Marta had been sitting next to, raised his arm. "Are you going to get a beer?"

Josh didn't bother answering. He was intent on following Marta from the noisy crowded room. She seemed to know where she was going. He was grateful, but uncomfortable not being in the lead. He'd never seen so many people in crisis in his life. At least not all in one place. For that matter, he'd never been in a hospital and was totally unprepared for the cloud of emotion and uncertainty that permeated the air like an ugly fog. Would Marta think less of him for not taking charge?

Her sure, quick steps led him down a hall and into an elevator. "I've spent a lot of time in a hospital very similar to this one." Marta punched a button on the wall and the elevator door slid shut. "My employer and friend, Mona, had to go in for chemotherapy a lot. Her husband couldn't always go along, so I accompanied her."

"This must bring back bad memories for you then." Josh wanted to reach out to her. She was staring straight ahead at the door, her back stiff. Something told him she wouldn't welcome his touch at that moment, though. Her total lack of facial expression suggested she was trying to hold her emotions in check. A bell rang and the car lurched to a stop.

Large signs in the corridor directed them to the surgery waiting room. The comfortable chairs and lack of noise contrasted powerfully with the chaos they'd just left. In fact, Josh was pleased to note there were only a few people who sat and talked quietly at the far end of the room. The receptionist's desk was empty so they took seats near a large bank of windows. Seattle's lights spread out below them and gave the night a festive appearance that didn't fit in with the reason they were there.

"Try not to worry." Marta reached across the armrest and grasped his hand.

Josh squeezed her hand in return, grateful she was there with him. The wait would have been intolerable without her. "I'm feeling more confident than when we first arrived. If she were dead or about to die, someone would have told us by now." He looked down at Marta's hand in his. It felt good, nestled there.

"That's just what I was thinking." She smiled as if trying to reassure him but the smile didn't reach her eyes. Marta turned away and stared out the window.

"Are you remembering other times you've waited in a hospital?"

Marta attempted to pull her hand from his, but he held it securely.

She spoke so quietly he could barely make out her words, "Yes. I hated it. Don't get me wrong . . . I wanted to be there for Mona, but each time she went to the hospital, the prognosis grew dimmer."

"I can't imagine what that must have been like for you." Josh stroked the back of her hand with the pad of his thumb. After a moment, he felt her relax. He could see her face reflected in the window and heard she exhale deeply at the same time her beautiful eyelashes dropped to a close. It took every ounce of his willpower to refrain from lifting her hand to his lips. If she were asleep, he'd chance it . . . just to be able to breathe in the fragrance of her skin. But she was awake. And he wasn't about to fool himself. The only reason she allowed even this small intimacy was their mutual love for Ginger.

A quiet rustle of movement behind him caused Josh to turn around. An older woman wearing a hospital name tag shuffled papers at the receptionist's desk. Picking up a clipboard, she moved toward Josh and Marta.

"And who are you waiting for?" The woman looked over the top of her reading glasses. Years of kindness and compassion had left lines etched on her face.

Josh cleared his throat. "Ginger Morton. My sister. Is there any word?"

The woman moved her index finger down the page she was holding. A frown creased her brow, but didn't detract from her pleasant countenance. "I don't see her name here. But that's not unusual. Most surgeries this time of night are unplanned so I don't always have an accurate list of names. Sit right here and I'll check for you."

Josh observed the woman as she walked back to her desk. She picked up the phone and spoke in low tones to some unknown person who had the power to bring this horrible wait to an end.

"Take a breath, Josh." He'd been concentrating so hard, Marta's voice made him jump.

"I guess my anxiety shows" he answered her. "She keeps looking over this way, so I know she's talking to someone about Ginny. Let's go over there."

"She said to wait," Marta objected, but rose from her chair just as Josh did.

The woman returned the phone to its cradle. Josh clutched Marta's hand which he'd clung to since they'd arrived. His eyes didn't leave the woman as he towed Marta toward the desk.

"Good news," the woman said pleasantly. "Your sister is out of surgery and will be taken to a room shortly. A doctor is on his way to speak to you."

Josh missed it if the woman said anything else. He whooped and pulled Marta into his arms. "She's OK! She must be OK, if they're taking her to a room."

Marta hugged him back. He kissed her forehead and held her tightly against his chest. Marta surprised Josh by not pulling away. If anything, she snuggled right into him. Euphoria spread through him, making him lightheaded. His sister was OK and Marta was in his arms. In about one more second though, she would realize how tightly he was holding her. He dropped his arms and stepped away. Marta's warm brown eyes shone with happiness and relief. It took her a moment to take a step back herself and when she did, Josh knew. Once again it hit home. She was never going to be his.

"Mr. Morton?" A man's voice intruded upon his longing.

"That's me." Josh turned and took in the man in green scrubs. "Are you Ginger's Doctor?"

"I'm Dr. Trump, the plastic surgeon on call tonight. Your sister had quite a fall, but she's doing well and you can see her now if you'd like."

"A fall? Do you know what happened? I guess I just assumed it was a car accident."

"The way she explained it, she slipped and fell. She broke her big toe, and will be laid up for a while till that mends. She also hit her head on the edge of a table. Had quite a nasty gash on her cheekbone. That's why they called me in. However, I expect that to mend rapidly and you won't even know the difference in a couple of months. In the meantime, she'll need someone to look after her till she gets used to walking with crutches. I'll want to keep her here overnight to rule out a concussion, but you can take her home tomorrow."

"I'll take care of her." Marta spoke up before Josh had a chance to say anything.

Josh avoided looking at her. "That won't be necessary. I'll hire someone to come in each day. And I can take care of her in the evening."

"Don't be ridiculous. I'm her best friend. I know how to take care of people. Ginger wouldn't want a stranger. Who better than me?"

"Well, you folks work it out between yourselves. Just so someone is around to make sure she doesn't put any weight on that toe. We couldn't put a cast on it, and it needs to be kept immobile. If you don't have any questions, I imagine you're anxious to see the patient." The doctor gestured for them to follow.

***

Marta trailed behind Josh and the doctor. What had gotten into Josh? Of *course* she was going to take care of Ginger. She'd have to juggle her schedule around a bit to take care of the apartments, but how hard could that be? Ginger's comfort came first. Didn't Josh trust her to take care of his sister?

She could hear snatches of conversation between Josh and the doctor as they strode down the hall ahead of her. She might as well have been invisible for all the attention they were paying her. The doctor was saying something about stitches and scarring. It was difficult to make out much more.

Marta had to break into a trot to keep up. Josh had evidently forgotten she was even with him. She trailed them around a corner and they all three entered a room. Josh immediately moved to the bed where Ginger rested with her head propped up on the pillows and one leg stuck out from under the covers. On her foot was a plastic shoe with some kind of wrapping holding it on.

Ginger's face lit up with a huge smile when she saw them. "Hi, you two. Hope I didn't drag you away from anything important to come here."

She ended her sentence with a huge wink that she so exaggerated, it looked more like a grimace. A large white bandage partially covered the left side of her face, from the hairline, to just above her jawbone. She flung her arms around Josh when he bent to kiss her forehead on the exposed side. Ginger nearly smacked him in the face with her flailing arms.

"Let go, you're choking me." Josh gently grasped her wrists and stepped back. "I'm relieved to see you're not seriously hurt."

"Hurt? Oh yeah, I got hurt, but I'm feeling just wonderful now." Her hand gestures seemed over magnified and she still wore a silly grin on her face.

Marta stood at the foot of the bed and watched the doctor check Ginger's pulse, look into her eyes with a penlight, and pat her shoulder. Glancing at Josh, she was glad to see the normal color had returned to his face. They'd both breathe easily now that they'd seen Ginger with their own eyes.

The Doctor turned to Josh. "I see no sign of a concussion, but she does seem pretty confused and disoriented. More so than we normally see from the amount of pain medication we gave her. The nursing staff will check on her every hour or so during the night." A beeping sound came from the Doctor's pocket and he pulled out a pager. "Well, I've got to go. Any questions?"

"Nope," Josh and Marta said in unison. Ginger didn't answer. She was holding her left hand outstretched, her palm facing away from her, singing "Diamonds Are a Girl's best Friend."

"Ginger." Josh waved his hand in front of her face, trying to get her attention. "Ginger . . . could you tell us how you fell?"

Marta moved around to the opposite side of the bed and looked questioningly at Josh. He met her eyes and shrugged his shoulders.

"Ginger. How did you fall? Do you remember?"

Ginger stopped singing long enough to answer exuberantly, "Of course I remember. I'll never forget it as long as I live." She flung her arm outward, barely missing Josh.

"I think Josh would like you to tell him what happened. I'm rather curious myself." Marta couldn't help smiling at Ginger's antics even though she was as impatient as Josh to hear her explanation.

"Oh, Marta. It was the most wonderful thing! There I was, in my most favorite Italian restaurant in the world, and I saw the most handsome man I've ever SEEN!" Ginger closed her eyes and clasped her hands to her chest in a mock swooning gesture.

Josh cleared his throat and tapped his fingers on his thighs. If he was doing it to hurry Ginger's story along, it wasn't working. She seemed determined to keep them both in suspense.

"Then what?"

Ginger's eyes flew open and she seemed surprised to see Josh and Martha at her bedside.

"Ginger." Josh said warningly, getting more fidgety by the moment.

Oh. Well, there I was. Walking through the dining room and there was this guy sitting there all alone eating that skinny spaghetti looking stuff. What is it called?"

"We don't care what some guy was eating," Josh growled. "How did you get hurt?"

"Just wait. I'm getting to that. You want to know how it happened don't you?"

Josh's sigh was distinctly audible from across the hospital bed where Marta stood waiting. He turned and pulled a chair to the bedside, clearly resigned to being there for a while.

"What did he look like?" Marta asked, trying to get Ginger talking again.

"Oh man. Who cares what he looked like? Ginger how did you get hurt?" Josh glowered at Marta.

Ginger's lower lip began to tremble. "Don't be mad, Josh. I'm trying to tell you how I fell."

"Well, at least now we're getting somewhere. You fell? In the restaurant?"

"Yes. That's what I'm trying to tell you. I was staring at this gorgeous hunk of a man and I didn't see the plate of food that some little kid knocked on the floor. Before I knew it, I slipped in some spaghetti sauce and hit the floor."

Marta couldn't help herself, she laughed out loud. "Well, that's one way to meet a guy. Did you get his name?"

"No. I must have been knocked out when I hit my head. The next thing I knew, the medics were loading me on a stretcher."

"So you went to all this trouble to get hurt and you didn't even get to meet the guy?"

"Oh, brother. I've heard enough. I'm going to go find some coffee." Josh rose from the chair and left the room, shaking his head.

"What's wrong with him?" Ginger seemed puzzled by Josh's departure. "Why did he ask me how I got hurt if he didn't want to know?"

Marta decided not to tell Ginger about the "bloody" clothing that had upset Josh so badly in the waiting room. She stifled a chuckle as she remembered his face just a moment ago when he realized how he'd overreacted to food stains. After all . . . they had both been worried out of their minds at the thought of Ginger being seriously injured. So worried they had fallen into each other's arms in relief when they received hopeful news about her condition.

Marta's face grew hot as she remembered the feel of Josh's arms around her. It had seemed so natural at the time. "People tend to get carried away by their emotions sometimes."

"What?"

Marta met Ginger's questioning gaze. "I think Josh just needed to get out and clear his head after being so worried about you." No way was she going to tell Ginger how she and Josh spent their time holding hands in the waiting room. She'd never hear the end of it.

"So tell me, Ginger. What was so great about this guy you fell for?"

"Fell for! Boy I sure did. I took one look at him and just knew. He's the one for me."

"Ginger, I don't want to rain on your parade, but isn't that a little impetuous? Did he give you any indication he felt the same way? Did you even get a chance to speak with each other?"

"Marta. You always were the practical one. We didn't have to speak. I saw him and I just *knew*. Now if I just knew his name, I'd find him and prove it to you."

"I guess if planning my life carefully means I'm practical, you're right. I don't plan on spending the rest of my life with a man when the only thing going for him is some weird chemical attraction I feel."

"Someday you're going to wake up and wish you'd followed your heart, Marta. I feel sorry for you."

"Don't feel sorry for me, Ginger. I know what it will take to make me happy and I know how to get it."

***

Josh returned to Ginger's hospital room just in time to hear Marta reinforce her resolve to change her life. So Ginger was right all along. Marta's heart was set on leaving them for greener pastures. Well, everyone deserved a chance to live their dream. Especially someone like Marta who had such a rough start in life. As much as he wanted to, he wasn't going to hold her back. In fact . . . he would do whatever he could to help her.

"You girls through talking about Ginger's dream man yet?" Josh smiled at both women as he handed a paper cup to Marta. She sat in the chair he had vacated, so he sat on the edge of Ginger's bed, being careful not to bump her foot.

"Actually Josh, I thought you'd want to hear all about him." Ginger smiled at her brother. "He's just the type of guy you'd pick out for me."

Josh chuckled. "Do you mean he's employed, doesn't have any tattoos, and can pass my background investigation?"

"Better than that. He'd look absolutely boring to you. Short hair. Button down collar. He even had a pocket protector and pens in his shirt pocket."

Josh peeked at Marta to gauge her reaction. As he suspected, her face reflected the surprise he felt at Ginger's description. One look at Ginger's face, though, showed she was dead serious.

Marta asked the question he was contemplating. "What exactly was it about him you liked, Ginger?"

"I looked at him and I *knew*. Underneath that nerdy facade beats the heart of a wild, passionate, caring, man."

"Yup. Just the kind of guy I was hoping my sister would bring home." Josh rolled his eyes for the benefit of the two women. It was time to stop this nonsense and get serious. "If you don't mind changing the subject, we need to discuss your care while you're mending from your accident."

"I've already told you, Josh. I'll take care of Ginger."

Josh looked Marta full in the face. "It's not that I don't think you're capable. You are. And it's obvious Ginger would be comfortable under your care. However, a promise is a promise. I told you I'd make sure you had time enough to job hunt. I don't expect you to delay your plans just to help us. This is a family matter and my responsibility. It won't be any trouble at all for me to find someone to come in and do the cooking and take care of Ginger till she's on her feet."

Marta turned her brown eyes on him. He could have sworn they'd doubled in size since he'd last looked. Maybe the unshed tears made them look bigger. He hadn't expected Marta to turn on the waterworks. That was more Ginger's style. Well, such an obvious feminine trick wouldn't sway him. If Marta felt obligated now to put aside her plans to care for Ginger, she would eventually resent him for letting her.

"Are you saying I'm not family? Ginger's like my sister."

"Of course, you're close. But it's not the same thing. I'm her brother. I'm perfectly capable of seeing she gets the proper care. You're a friend from her childhood . . . a good friend. But, there's no duty that comes with that." Josh folded his arms across his chest, hoping the gesture would stave off an argument.

Marta threw a glance toward Ginger, who for once remained silent. She looked back at Josh. He could plainly see the puzzlement on her face. Was she going to protest some more? If she did, should he give in? After all, she was right. She was the perfect choice as Ginny's care giver. No. Everything Marta had done since she'd arrived had shown her single mindedness toward one goal. That of leaving her past as far behind as possible. In the end, Josh and Ginger would only be reminders of the childhood Marta wanted to forget.

Marta stiffened. "I think Ginger should be the one to-"

"My mind is made up, Marta." Josh jerked his head toward Ginger who had drifted off to sleep. "She wouldn't want you to give up your plans for her. Haven't you made her feel badly enough?"

"Wh-what do you mean?"

"I mean, you've made Ginger feel she was somehow less than you because she's different. Did you ever once think about her feelings while you were prancing around the apartment in your fancy, high-society clothes?"

"I never-"

"That's right. You never. Never thought about anybody but yourself. The longer you stay around, the more you're going to hurt my sister when you leave. You might as well start cutting the cord now."

"You don't understand." Marta's lower lip trembled as she spoke. "I never intended to turn my back on her."

"No? How was she going to fit in with your new friends? Were you going to make her over too? She doesn't care about the same things you do." Josh cut off his sermon. It broke his heart to see Marta's pain from the hurt he inflicted on her. He wanted to take it all back. Ask her to stay. Beg her to stay. Yeah, right. Like she'd *ever* be happy with the life he could offer her.

"I didn't realize you felt that way, Josh."

Josh averted his eyes from Marta's quivering lips. He stood and crumpled the empty coffee container in his hand. "Ginger looks like she's out for the night. It's late. Come on, I'll drive you home. Tomorrow's going to be a busy day." He strode out of the room and down the hall toward the elevator. His jaw clenched and he kept his face turned away from.her She thought he didn't understand. He understood. A lot more than she gave him credit for.

114

CHAPTER TEN

Marta slammed the door behind the woman she'd just fired. Josh would throw a fit when he found out, but she didn't care. The old battle-ax had spent more time watching TV than caring for Ginger. Sheesh! She hadn't even bothered to cook Ginger a hot lunch. Granted, Ginger hadn't complained. The baloney sandwich and cola she'd received was as good as the meals she used to cook for herself. Marta stomped into the kitchen and yanked one of Josh's copper pots off the rack.

She pulled a towel out of the drawer and tied it around her waist to protect her linen skirt. There was no time to change from her going-to-an-interview clothes if she was going to get dinner ready in time. Did Josh think the woman he'd hired from the nursing agency was going to take care of it? Had he even checked her credentials or asked for references? Probably not. He must have hired her sight unseen.

Marta slammed a yellow onion onto the cutting board. Using a knife from the set Josh recently bought, she sliced both ends, ripped the paper-like peel off and threw it in the sink. If Josh hadn't been in such an all-fire hurry to get rid of her, he could have been more cautious about whom he hired. This last woman wasn't any better than the first one he'd picked. Ginger, bless her heart, hadn't complained to Josh about either of them. Yep, Josh was not going to be happy about her interfering in his family business again. He'd made it abundantly clear that night at the hospital he considered her an outsider. It still hurt to remember how he thought she wasn't concerned enough to care for Ginger.

She reached for the cleaver and fiercely sliced and chopped the onion into quarter-inch chunks. Tears poured down her cheeks and her nose began to run. The hot oil in the pan popped when she scooped up the onion and dumped it in. Marta bent forward so she could wipe her eyes with the hem of her make-shift apron. The last thing she needed was for Josh to return and find her with red watery eyes again. At least this time she had a good excuse so she wouldn't have to watch his face flush with guilt for hurting her.

Marta added some crushed garlic to sauté along with the onion. At least Josh had the decency to feel bad about what he'd said, even if he meant the words. *Not a member of the family.* How many times had she heard that when she was growing up? But it had never defeated her and it wasn't going to defeat her now. She didn't care what Josh thought. She had to do what her heart told her. If that included taking care of Ginger right now, that's what she'd do . . . no matter what Mr. Perfect, Josh Morton, the Dictator, thought about it. Marta sniffed. Loudly. How could he even think she would put herself ahead of her best friend?

"Marta?" Ginger's voice rang out from the living room where she was lying on the couch with her leg elevated.

Marta wiped her eyes again and poked her head around the corner. "You called?"

"I have to go to the bathroom. Could you hand me those crutches? Please? They're clear on the other side of the room."

"Of course. But let me walk with you. You still don't have the hang of walking with them. I'm afraid you'll slip."

"It's been a week since the accident. You'd think I would have learned to use them by now."

Marta smiled fondly at her friend. Ginger hated asking for help. In fact she'd been a model patient. At least during those times Josh risked leaving them alone together. "It's not as easy as it looks when you see other folks walk with them. I'm sure you'll catch on soon." She handed the crutches to her friend and helped her up from the couch.

Indeed, Ginger had not gotten the hang of it when it came to using the crutches. Marta had adjusted them and readjusted them the last week, trying to find the right fit.

Still, Ginger usually dropped one to the floor after taking just a few steps. Marta sympathized with Ginger's frustration and tried to help her friend maneuver around the small apartment whenever necessary.

"You're improving every time you try. Once you get that bandage off your face and can use both eyes again, maybe you won't bump into the walls as much."

"That reminds me . . . "Ginger paused to get a better grip on her crutches. "I have an appointment to get the stitches out tomorrow. Since you don't drive, and you fired my nurse, how am I going to get there? I hate to ask Josh. He's got so much to do."

Marta cringed inwardly. One more reason for Josh to be upset over Marta's firing this last woman. He'd already used her lack of driving ability as an excuse for hiring a stranger to care for Ginger. Not that he needed another reason. He apparently carried an itemized list of her lack of qualifications around in his head, dragging them all out to justify getting rid of her. She puzzled over his abrupt change of heart where she was concerned. First he hadn't wanted her there, then he appeared to be doing everything he could to keep her, and now he acted as if he couldn't wait for her to get out of his apartment and life. It made her dizzy to think about it.

"Don't worry, Ginger. I'll take you there. I'll call a cab."

Ginger leaned one of her crutches against the wall and turned her head toward Marta. "I can't let you do that. A cab would be way too expensive."

"I insist on getting the cab." Marta knew Ginger was going to be on a tight budget for a long time since she didn't have a health insurance plan that would cover all her hospital and doctor bills. "You know, that restaurant should pay for some of your bills. After all, if they'd cleaned up that mess on the floor, you wouldn't have slipped. Why don't you let me call them?"

"No. They'll just say if I hadn't been gawking at that hunk, and if I hadn't been wearing my new platform shoes, I probably wouldn't have fallen."

"Well, if that's the way you want it, but it wouldn't hurt to ask." Marta closed the door for Ginger. "Let me know when you're ready to come out."

Once Ginger was safely in the bathroom, Marta returned to the kitchen to finish dinner preparations. The onions were a little overdone, but not burned. A couple cans of stewed tomatoes dumped in the pan, added a new aroma. She pulled a round steak from the refrigerator and dredged it in flour. After seasoning the steak with salt and pepper, Marta zealously pounded it with the back of the cleaver to tenderize it.

The kitchen door creaked open behind her. "I didn't expect you home so soon. I see you've started dinner." Josh's voice sounded sharp enough to tenderize the toughest cut of meat.

Marta put down the cleaver and turned to him, fixing him with a glare. "Your high paid care giver wasn't expecting me either. I surprised her snoozing on the couch."

"What? Well, I'll call her right now and tell her there'll be no more of that."

"Darn right. I fired her."

"Now just a minute! I told you the last time to stop interfering." Josh glared back and wagged his index finger in her face. "If there was a problem, you should have come to me with it."

Marta stood her ground. "You're just mad because it was me that told her to leave. You would have done the same thing, Josh."

"Maybe. And maybe not. It was my call. Not yours."

Marta bristled. "If you had let me take care of her like I wanted to in the beginning, we wouldn't even be having this argument."

"Is that what this is about? You keep making up excuses to fire these women just to get back at me because you didn't get your own way?"

Ginger's call for help put a stop their quarrel, but Marta knew that wouldn't be the end of it.

"I'll go help her," Josh murmured through gritted teeth.

"Fine." Marta picked up the cleaver and launched a steady pounding of the steak till a cloud of flour floated over the counter. What was she going to have to do to get through to him? She couldn't decide if she was angry or hurt, but Josh's attitude was going to have to change. She tossed the meat pieces into the pan with the sauce and covered it all with a tight fitting lid. Wiping her hands on her makeshift apron, she stalked into the living room ready to do battle.

Josh had settled Ginger in his recliner and was adjusting the footrest to elevate her leg. Seeing the affection he showed his sister brought new moisture to Marta's eyes. He had showed her the same tenderness when she'd had that bad allergic reaction. And now he acted like he hated her. Granted, he had been right in a couple of his accusations, but hadn't he ever heard of a thing called forgiveness?

Ginger looked from Marta to Josh anxiously. "Marta is fixing Swiss steak. Doesn't it smell good, Josh?"

Marta, who had moments before set out to give Josh a dressing down, stopped. It would do no good to argue in front of Ginger. It would only get her upset. If there was one thing Marta had learned, Ginger had an obsessive wish for Marta and her brother to get along. She watched Josh lean over and give Ginger a quick kiss on her temple, then playfully ruffle her hair. A lump rose in her throat. How lucky Ginger was to be loved like that.

Josh straightened and gave Marta a look that gave her a chill. "It's too late to call the employment agency today, so I've got no choice but to have you stay here with Ginger tomorrow."

"That won't be a problem for me, Josh. I'll see to it she gets to her doctor appointment and I'll meet with the tenants association when we get home." Marta pivoted and quickly moved to the kitchen before anyone saw the tears seeping from her eyes.

***

The next day, Josh completed only half his usual workload. He stopped often, finding excuses to go near the apartment to get a glimpse of Marta. He wasn't very proud of himself for the way he'd been treating her lately. In fact it was a real effort to keep up this ridiculous pretense of not wanting her around. He felt downright mean. Especially when her beautiful lips trembled as if she were about to cry. If only he could stop their quivering by covering them with a hard kiss.

He made another trip to the tool shed, glancing again toward the apartment. Had they come back from the doctor's office yet? If it were summertime instead of late fall, the front door would be open to let the outside air in. With the wind blowing the threat of a rainstorm around, everyone's apartment doors and windows were closed tight. He ducked inside the shed and picked up another two gallons of paint. He should apologize to her. Ask her forgiveness and tell her he wanted her to stay. But she'd agree. Marta would stay, out of guilt and her feelings of responsibility toward Ginger, if for no other reason. And every day she stayed, made it harder and harder for him to keep his real feelings to himself. In the end, they'd both be unhappy. No, he had to stick to his resolve and send her on her way.

When Josh left the shed, carrying a can of paint in each hand, he spotted Marta helping Ginger up the steps. Before he could set the paint on the ground and go help, a group of tenants appeared and helped her inside. Josh heard Marta's laughter as they all disappeared through the door. Laughter that grew silent when he was around. He missed it. Gripping the handles on the cans, he turned in the opposite direction.

120

Josh angrily deposited the paint cans on the floor of apartment 4B. Marta had dressed up again. She must have combined another job interview with the trip to the doctor. Why she hadn't found a job yet was beyond his understanding. Anyone in their right mind should be glad to have her on their payroll. If they'd only call him, he'd be glad to give her a glowing recommendation. But no one had called and asked. Had she even given his name as a reference? Or had she been ashamed of working for him? It didn't take a mental giant to figure out the answer to that one.

His gut churned and twisted at the thought of spending any more time sharing an apartment with a woman whose smile turned him inside out. How many nights could he lie in bed knowing she was just on the other side of the wall? How long would it be before he gave up and dragged her into his arms? Josh licked his lips to ease their dryness. It would be only a matter of time before Marta figured out his feelings. She would never do anything as unkind as laugh. Not Marta, who treated everyone with kindness. No . . . she'd even try and hide the pity she'd feel when she realized he loved her. The sudden realization of how strong that love was, slammed Josh in the gut like a fist.

Josh walked over to the window, looked out toward the apartment he shared with the two women he cared about most in the world and made a decision.

***

Marta gathered up the coffee mugs and paper napkins left behind by the tenants, and carried them to the kitchen. She smiled, remembering how well the meeting had gone. They had agreed on a neighborhood watch program. The tenants then identified kids whose parents worked, and a stay at home mom had volunteered to be the "latchkey" home where kids could go in the event of trouble. The tenants were slowly becoming a close-knit community and expressed pride in keeping the newly remodeled apartments looking neat and clean. A committee, who named themselves The Maple Vista Beautification Society, had been elected as the watchdogs of all the outdoor areas. They would not only inspect the grounds for vandalism and litter, but planned to plant marigolds along all the sidewalks the following spring.

Marta washed and rinsed the cups, placing them in the drainer to dry. Josh would be pleased with her report of today's meeting. If the residents followed through in taking responsibility for their neighborhood, everyone would benefit, including Josh and Ginger.

The thump thump of crutches approached the kitchen. "You were right, Marta. Who would've thought a bandage over my eye would make such a big difference to my walking skills. I made it to the bathroom and back without anyone's help. Ginger's wide smile lit up her entire face.

"Good for you. Josh will be so pleased with your progress." Marta hurriedly pulled a kitchen chair out for her friend. "Do you feel up to keeping me company while I fix dinner? It's been a long day for you."

"Absolutely. But give me something to do, please. I'm sick of just sitting around watching TV." She plopped down on the chair and slid the crutches under the table.

Marta pulled salad makings from the refrigerator and placed them on the table in front of Ginger. Then she added a bowl and paring knife. "These greens have already been washed. They only need to be cut or chopped."

Judging by the rustling around in the living room, Josh had come in for the evening. He usually came right to the kitchen to check the dinner menu and filch a cookie or two from the jar Marta kept on the counter. Tonight, however, he apparently had phone calls to make. Marta could hear the creak of his recliner and the low murmur of his voice. It wasn't like him to not at least say hello when he came home. Marta took a step toward the living room, but thought better of it and went back to her dinner preparations.

Lately the atmosphere had grown so strained between them, even Miss Treymore had remarked on it. When Marta and Josh weren't avoiding each other, they seemed to be at each other's throats. Marta measured out enough of Josh's favorite coffee to make a pot for dinner. After she poured the cold water in the well and flipped on the switch she moved to the doorway to see if he was still on the phone. He didn't even glance up. Not wanting to appear to be eavesdropping, she retreated to the safety of the kitchen.

"Did I hear Josh come in?" Ginger stopped chopping long enough to look to Marta for an answer.

"You did. He's on the phone."

"That's odd. There must be an emergency. I expected him to come right in here and quiz me on my doctor's visit."

Marta didn't tell Ginger her suspicions that Josh wasn't neglecting her but rather avoiding Marta. Perhaps she should have a talk with Josh . . . find out what his problem was. The tension between them caused her stomach to knot each time they shared the same room. At one time, she would have shrugged it off because she knew that soon she wouldn't have to see him at all. But now . . . they had become friends. Or sort of. She thought they had reached a mutual appreciation for each other. *She* certainly wanted to be friends. If only he wasn't so moody lately.

Marta patted Ginger's shoulder on her way to the silverware drawer. "Maybe he finally realizes he's your brother, not your father." *Now wouldn't that be a switch? What would Josh do if he wasn't trying to run everybody's life for them? Well, not everybody's. Just her and Ginger's lives.*

"He cares. How many people are as lucky as I am?" Ginger's tone of voice sounded happy rather than defensive. "Some people have nobody to care about them."

Marta stopped in her tracks. Boy didn't she know it? Who had ever really cared about her? Besides Ginger and Mona? And Mona was gone.

"It's a two-way street, Ginger. You love Josh a lot, too." A two-way street. Marta glanced toward the living room. She should take the first step. *She* would make things right between herself and Ginger's brother.

No sooner had the thought crossed her mind, than Josh came into the kitchen and planted a kiss on Ginger's head. "Looks like you're feeling a lot better today." He gently lifted her chin with his fingers. "The doc was right. There's only a little line where he put those stitches in your face. I'll bet even that disappears in no time."

Marta set the mismatched dinner plates on the table with a clatter. Did Josh even notice her presence? She moved a chair, letting the legs annoyingly scrape across the floor. He didn't even look up. He was examining Ginger's face as if the slightly yellowish hue under her eye was the most fascinating sight in the world. Was this what the future held? Josh treating her like a nonperson for the remaining time she lived there?

"Ahem." Marta stiffened her back. Putting one hand on her hip.

Josh glanced toward her and raised an eyebrow when he noticed her piercing stare. "Did you say something?"

Of all the . . . Marta gestured toward the table with her free hand. "Would you mind moving? I'm trying to get ready for dinner."

Josh lazily stepped away from the table, pinning Marta in place with a hard stare. "I'm glad you're here. I've got some news for you."

"News?" Marta braced herself for Josh's news. His impersonal tone of voice suggested it was not good news. So much for burying the hatchet.

"I've found a job for you."

"A job?" Marta searched his face for any expression that might reveal his thoughts. She might as well have been looking at a post. Was this job a good thing? Or not?

"Yeah. You haven't had much luck finding a job suitable enough for you, so I made a few phone calls and I think I've found one you'll like."

Marta bristled at Josh's audacity. He had interfered in her life. Again. And he sounded sarcastic about her preferences to boot. "I don't recall asking for your help."

"Well, you got it." Josh interrupted her before she could tell him what he could do with the job he'd found for her.

Ginger tapped a spoon on the table. "Can't you two be in the same room for five minutes without being at each other's throats?"

Marta flushed guiltily. Ginger stated exactly what she had been thinking earlier. She'd acted like a spoiled kid. Of course she had been looking for a good job. She should at least listen to what Josh had to say before telling him the job he found wasn't what she'd been looking for.

She took a deep breath and attempted to arrange her face in a grateful expression. "I'm sorry, Josh. Tell me about this job."

"I called a friend of mine who's the service manager at a car dealership over in Bellevue."

Marta frowned. What had he done? Found her a job as a mechanic?

Josh continued, apparently oblivious to Marta's chagrin. "It seems they need a receptionist for the sales floor."

Marta gulped and tried to get her mouth working to form a response. Josh was serious. He thought she'd go to work in some grubby garage in Timbuktu. He must really want to get rid of her.

Ginger spoke up. "Isn't that where your friend Rick works? The company where they sell all those fancy limousines?"

Marta's ears pricked up. Limousines? "Where, exactly is this place?"

Ginger looked concerned. "Bellevue is over on the other side of Lake Washington. Quite a long way from here."

"It's not so far," Josh quickly assured her. "I'm sure there's a bus route that would take Marta there until she finds a place in Bellevue to live."

"But-"

"This is what Marta's been looking for. A good paying job in a good area. I asked and the pay is very good." Josh's voice contained an edge of impatience.

"Stop discussing me as if I weren't here. It's my decision, after all." Was the opposite side of Lake Washington far enough away as far as Josh was concerned? "Do you have a phone number for me to call to arrange an interview?"

"It's all taken care of. You have an appointment with the manager tomorrow morning. I'll drive you there."

Marta opened her mouth and quickly clamped it shut again. So what if Josh seemed to be pushing her out. Wasn't this what she wanted?

"Say something." Josh glowered at her. "This is what you want isn't it?"

Was it? Marta groaned inwardly. Now that the time to move on neared, her insides knotted in fear. Which was ridiculous. What was there to be afraid of, anyway? She'd planned for this. Her life would be wonderful. She'd already paid her dues, lived on the streets, exposed herself to danger; what was left to fear?

"Of course it's what I want. I've never made a secret of it, have I?" A cramp seized Marta's stomach and she covered it with both hands.

"Good," Josh said curtly, "Be ready to leave right after breakfast." He turned, and without another word, strode from the room.

***

Josh turned on the shower and adjusted it to the hottest setting he could stand. The sound of the water beating on his head drowned the conversation from the other part of the apartment, but didn't do much to drown his thoughts. Nor did the steam surrounding him erase the memory of Marta's puzzled expression when he'd told her about the job. Did she honestly think he *wanted* her to leave? Letting her go, tore his heart up, but would make her happiest in the long run. Josh lathered himself, scrubbing his skin twice as

126

hard as necessary. If he rubbed himself raw with steel wool, it wouldn't be enough to get his mind off the scene in the kitchen. And his part in it.

At least the job he'd found her would insure she worked for decent people. They would pay her well and treat her with respect. Most importantly, he'd be able to keep tabs on her.

Ginger would miss Marta. So would half the tenants in the apartments. Face it, everybody would miss her. He'd be lucky if nobody moved out when they heard they'd have to deal with him instead of Marta. He wrenched the hot water handle to the off position, which caused needles of icy water to spray over him. He flinched and shut the cold off too.

Josh stepped from the shower and grabbed a towel off the rack. Driving Marta to her interview would serve two purposes. The first, of course, would be to help her out. More importantly, it would give him a chance to speak to his good friend, Rick. He'd make Rick promise to watch out for her and report back to him. What better way to guarantee her safety?

CHAPTER ELEVEN

Marta twirled around and around, till she collapsed, laughing, on her bed. A job. She finally had a job that would propel her into the life of her dreams. Who would have thought it would be found in such an unlikely place? A car dealership. But not just any cars, these were luxury cars. Cars that cost as much as a small house. She rolled over onto her stomach and rested her chin on her hands. She tried to imagine a more elegant workplace, but even by squeezing her eyes shut, she couldn't.

Her new job would make it possible for her to meet some of the most prestigious people in the entire Seattle area. Hers would be the first face they'd see as they entered the plush carpeted showroom. Soft background music in the beautifully decorated room filled with plants and freshly cut flowers, created an atmosphere befitting even the pickiest consumers. Marta's new responsibilities included making potential customers comfortable and conducting the initial interview which would identify their preferences in automobile styles. Only then, would they be turned over to an immaculately groomed sales representative. And, not a spot of grease anywhere in sight.

Marta reached for the packet of information she'd brought home. Her new boss said it contained everything she needed to know about the high-priced automobiles he sold. She'd have to memorize every detail. He'd said it wouldn't be enough to be charming and beautiful, although his eyes had signaled he approved of her in that area. No, she'd be required to be knowledgeable about different models, options and available color choices. Even though she wouldn't be directly involved in a sale, her deportment, even a small remark, could affect the outcome of a potential client's visit.

Glancing through the glossy brochures, Marta saw she had a lot of studying to do. Nothing in her background prepared her for discussing the array of accessories or equipment available on these fancy automobiles. And when it came to engine specifications, she couldn't decipher anything she'd read so far. Marta hated the thought of asking Josh for help, again, but it looked as if she had no choice. She had never even driven a car, let alone contemplated purchasing one. If she had, her budget probably wouldn't have included a choice of metallic exterior colors. She giggled. Josh's pickup wasn't exactly a royal metallic indigo color either.

Marta frowned. Would she be able to learn all this before reporting to work the following Monday? Josh had dropped her off at the apartment and disappeared. It could be hours before he returned. She'd memorize the brochures describing colors and upholstery choices first. Then she'd cook Josh's favorite foods for dinner. That would be the easy part. Josh liked everything. But would he spend time helping her? After giving up most of his morning to drive her clear to Bellevue? He'd been strangely silent on the way home.

Running her finger down the list of exterior colors, she raised an eyebrow. Three different colors of black? Who thought up that idea? Wasn't black just that? Black? At least there weren't more than a dozen color names to memorize. Marta imagined the look on Josh's face when she told him about this. His blue eyes would get those crinkly lines around them, like when he got ready to laugh, but trying to hold it back. Then his mouth would kind of turn up at the corners and twitch a little . . . right before he would say in all seriousness, "a car to match your black eye, huh?"

Now for the interior colors. Oh, no. There weren't as many, but some were only available on certain car models. Should she memorize the model numbers first? And wouldn't she need to somehow match the model numbers with the styles? Yep, this could provide an entire evening's entertainment for Josh. She might as well get prepared for his teasing. For once she wouldn't mind.

***

Josh's teeth jarred from the hammer's force as it hit the wall . . . enough force to leave a dent in the plasterboard. The damage barely registered in his brain as he moved from one panel to another. He would mud over the holes when he went back over the room with joint tape. Nearly every wall needed replacing. The former residents of the apartment had trashed it. The living room and bedroom looked as if someone had put their fist through the plaster in several places. Could it have been someone who had fallen victim to a woman with beautiful brown eyes?

A man could easily lose control over the wrong woman if he wasn't careful. But then, any woman was the wrong one if she created that kind of frustration. Josh picked up a roll of tape and applied it along the seams between the new drywall. He'd mud it over and let it dry a day before coming back with a sander. He was a week ahead of the schedule he'd set for himself. Marta would be pleased for him when he told her. But would there be any point of even saying anything to her? Right now, her mind only focused on dreams up in the clouds.

Josh clenched his fist. He had figured she'd be happy about the job. He *wanted* her to be happy. Why else had he gone out on a limb and asked a favor from a business acquaintance? He just never expected her to be so ecstatic about it. That's all she'd talked about on the drive home. Her fabulous new job. The plush surroundings she'd be working in. The important people she'd be meeting. She'd never sounded that excited about working for him. He hated her new job. He must never let on to Marta, though.

Two hours later, Josh let himself into the apartment he still shared with Ginger and Marta. A smarter man would move out right away, but he couldn't. Ginger still walked with crutches and might need him. He needed to keep an eye on Marta, too . . . just in case her new job didn't work out.

He didn't altogether trust Rick to give him accurate updates. He couldn't very well call every week and ask her new boss; that would jeopardize Marta's working relationship with him. No, he'd wait it out, staying in the apartment, no matter how uncomfortable it became.

Evidently Marta's enthusiasm hadn't waned during the last couple of hours. Josh could hear the zeal in her voice as she talked to Ginger in the kitchen. Miss Treymore's voice chimed in too, no doubt dispensing her own unique brand of advice. Maybe he could sneak into the bathroom for a shower before they knew he'd come in.

"Josh."

No such luck. Marta poked her head around the corner and motioned him into the kitchen. He saw she'd changed into a hip hugging pair of jeans and T-shirt since he'd dropped her off.

"Come in here. I just told Miss Treymore about my new job and how you arranged for my interview and drove me there. You are such a sweetheart. I'm so happy I could hug you."

Marta rushed toward him and threw her arms around his neck before he had a chance to escape. He burned everywhere her body touched his as she tightened her hold on him. He wanted to thrust her away. Why couldn't she leave him alone? Couldn't she see what she did to him?

Miss Treymore came out of the kitchen, and Ginger followed, her crutches thumping on the floor. "Young man," she pointed her cane at him for emphasis, "That's a wonderful thing you did for our Marta. I bet you'll regret it though. She's the best assistant manager you've ever had."

Josh curled his fingers around Marta's wrists and removed her arms from around his neck. She was darn lucky the other two women were present. His willpower wouldn't have held if they'd been alone. He would've returned the embrace . . . pulled her in tight and kissed her till her lips were bruised.

"Needless to say, she's the only assistant manager I've ever had." Josh took a step back, nearly knocking a lamp off the end table. Did she get some perverted thrill out of teasing him?

"Josh, I hate to ask you . . . you've already done so much. But would you help me go over these auto brochures tonight?" She still stood so close to him he could feel the heat emanating from her body.

Josh gritted his teeth. "Can't Ginger help you?" He looked toward his sister for help.

"Gee, Josh, I'd like to, but Miss Treymore and I are going to that new lingerie store at the mall and then we're going to swing by the restaurant where I fell and have a bite of dessert." She exchanged conspiratorial looks with the older woman. "Maybe that hunk eats there on a regular basis."

Josh shook his head. Ginger had completely ignored the pleading look he'd given her. "How are you planning on getting there? You can't drive with that cast."

"George is driving us, of course."

Josh turned and looked at his neighbor, who'd spoken. "George?"

"George Whitestone. The mailman." Miss Treymore winked at Ginger, who was apparently in on the plan. "I thought he'd enjoy the lingerie shop. Maybe he'd like to advise me on my purchases."

"George? You're taking him lingerie shopping?" Josh chuckled at the thought of their mailman following the two women around the mall. Every man's nightmare

Miss Treymore drew herself up indignantly. "There's no need to use that tone, young man. George doesn't qualify for geezerhood quite yet. In fact, we're planning on going on a little trip. Naturally I'd like his opinion on what I should take." She patted her silver curls and sent another wink in Ginger's direction.

Josh looked from Miss Treymore, to Ginger, and then to Marta. Could the old lady be serious? A romance between her and the mailman? And Ginger wanted to pursue the man responsible for her accident? A person would think spring had sprung, rather than the first nips of winter. Did everyone have a love life except him?

Marta still had her gaze locked on him, waiting for an answer. Evidently she'd rather stay home than go lingerie shopping with the others. Josh shifted his weight to his left foot, leaned against the wall and crossed his right foot over at the ankle. Visions of Marta in the lingerie shop fueled his imagination. He knew exactly which store they'd been talking about. The ads had run on the local television station. Josh shifted his weight back to the other leg. Bits of red and black lace made up the lingerie the TV models wore. No flannel pajamas or thermo underwear there, just little bitty ribbon straps and see-through gauze. He cleared his throat.

"I really don't think I'd be much help, Marta-"

"Oh, please." Marta batted her thick lashes at him. Now where'd she learned a trick like that? Dang woman.

"Can't you wait till-?"

The sound of a honking horn interrupted Josh's protests. Ginger swung her crutches around and followed Miss Treymore to the front door. She looked back once. "Marta would you like us to pick up something for you while we're out?"

Miss Treymore cackled. "Yeah, like one of those push-up bras for your first day at work?"

"No!" Josh burst out without thinking. Did they think Marta's new job was in a strip joint? He glared at the retreating women. All three of them laughed. What was so darn funny? Maybe it was a good thing he'd have time with Marta while the other two were out. He could warn her about sexual harassment on the job. "Fancy underwear, indeed," he muttered.

"Did you say something?" Marta closed the door behind the others and turned toward him.

"Nothing. I didn't say anything." Josh pursed his lips. To think he'd worried Marta would be a bad influence. His sister and her new best friend could use some lessons in good conduct.

"Ginny and I have eaten already, but I saved plenty for you. Why don't you wash up and I'll heat up your dinner?"

Josh nodded and headed to the bathroom. What color lingerie would Marta buy if she'd gone? He'd never had to duck and fight his way around drying undies in the bathroom like his married friends did. If any silky underthings had hung from the shower rod, he'd have noticed the color right away. How could he possibly concentrate on helping Marta study for work with all their lingerie talk? Sometimes they treated him like he wasn't there. Women.

***

Marta watched Josh finish a second piece of lemon meringue pie. He'd hardly said a word during his meal. Once when she'd brushed his arm while pouring him a cup of coffee, he'd yanked his arm away as if he'd been burned. "Would you like another cup of coffee?"

He licked his fork clean and wiped his mouth with a napkin. "No thanks. I'm stuffed. You should have saved the dishes for me. I know you've had a long day and still have studying to do."

Marta narrowed her eyes and studied him. He'd begun speaking to her only in a monotone. Why? He'd never struck her as the moody type, but lately he'd been impossible to figure out. If only she could do something to cheer him up. He'd done so much for her. Even his favorite foods had failed to make him smile. Not that he'd been rude. He said, "Thank you" at all the right times, but his heart remained elsewhere.

"You know, once all the apartments are rented, there wouldn't have been enough to keep me busy around here. This job couldn't have come at a better time."

"Um."

"What?"

"Nothing."

134

Marta cleared the remaining dishes from the table. Nothing? He'd grunted. Couldn't he do any better than that? Did she dare broach the subject of him helping her again? But if he didn't help her, she'd never figure all that engine stuff out. Josh rose from the table. Any minute he'd leave the apartment or, if he stayed, he'd immerse himself in a TV program or paperwork. Josh stood as if readying himself to escape. Marta needed to get his attention and keep it. Now.

"Ginger seems determined to hunt down and meet the man she saw at the restaurant that night." Marta waited for a reaction. Josh's hands gripped the back of the chair and he slid it close to the table. His gaze darted toward the doorway as if his sister would materialize any moment.

Receiving no response, Marta continued, "Wouldn't it be something if she actually found him? Knowing Ginger, she'd capture him and have an engagement ring on her finger in a matter of weeks. Why, the way things are going, you might have this entire apartment to yourself before you know it."

Josh turned and glared at her. Not the reaction she'd hoped for, but at least she'd gotten his attention. Marta noticed how dark his blue eyes became when he got all perturbed. Oops. Maybe she shouldn't have insinuated Ginger might move away. Josh proprietary attitude toward his sister bordered on obsessive.

"If my sister finds the right man, I'll be glad to give my blessing." Josh's words were clipped, his countenance immobile. He gave no clues to whatever thoughts roamed his mind, but it appeared as if he had distanced himself from Marta, Ginger, and even his own emotions. Suddenly he took a step toward her and grasped her chin between his thumb and forefinger. "Not the answer you expected, was it? Are you trying to get my goat for some reason? If so, I'd like to know what that reason is."

The suddenness of Josh's confrontation startled her. She should have known better than tease him about his sister. No father could be more protective of a daughter than Josh was of Ginger. Yet he'd let her go this evening without an argument. His behavior didn't add up.

"Well?" Josh tipped her chin upward, forcing her to look into his eyes. She wanted to avert her eyes away from his steady gaze, but that would be admitting he had the power to make her uncomfortable. And who wouldn't be disturbed by the smoldering emotion she saw on his face? Fright rose in her throat from somewhere deep in the core of her. His touch burned her chin where he still held her fast. How silly to feel so apprehensive. Josh was her friend. Why did she feel paralyzed then, unable to take even one step away from his touch? What could there possibly be to fear?

As swiftly as he'd captured her, he dropped his hand from her face, his mouth widening in an unnatural smile. Marta exhaled, realizing she'd been holding her breath. She clutched her hands together so Josh wouldn't see they were shaking. What was the matter with her, anyway? She acted nearly as strange as Josh. Must be a full moon out. No other explanation made sense.

"Maybe I'll have a cup of coffee after all. I want to be alert if I'm going to help you study." He delivered the announcement as if nothing at all had happened between them. Relieved, Marta got the coffee out of the cupboard and pulled out the coffee maker. Her hands stopped shaking as soon as she gave them something to do. She must have imagined the electrical charge that had coursed through her only moments before. Her hormones probably were cycling and making her crazy. It happened to people all the time.

"Show me what you're studying." He ran both hands down his Jean clad thighs.

The gesture drew Marta's attention to the way the worn denim looked on him. A prickling sensation spread through her torso, creating small electrical charges that shot to her limbs and clear to her fingertips and toes. She quickly averted her eyes. It was one thing to appreciate a perfect male form and quite another to dwell on those attributes when she had no intention at all of enjoying them.

She placed the stack of brochures on the table. "Uh, why don't you sit back down?" At least seated, he wouldn't distract her as much, not to mention less likely to escape. She took the seat next to him, scooting up close so she could follow along as he read the material. The tangy citrus scent of his aftershave tickled her nose. For a man who worked with his hands, he kept himself surprisingly well groomed when off the job. Marta looked at his clothing. His plaid flannel shirts may not be the height of fashion, but were always clean. He probably wore coveralls over his clothes today and then removed them before entering the apartment. Any other man would have tracked drywall dust from the front door to the shower. Not Josh. He nearly always showed consideration that way.

Josh ran his index finger down the list of vehicle options, stopping to explain the ones Marta didn't understand. Even the fingernails at the end of his strong blunt fingers were clean. Marta stared at the fine hairs barely visible on back of his hands. She looked at her own hands, mentally comparing the differences between the way a man and woman were created.

"Are you listening to me?" Josh's deep voice penetrated her thoughts.

"Wh-what? Of course I'm listening. My mind just wandered a little for a moment there."

"It must have strayed to a place you liked, judging by the little smile on your face."

Startled, Marta looked into his eyes. He'd been looking at her face? If so, he knew she'd been staring at his hands. He met her gaze, one eyebrow quizzically raised. She didn't know what to say. Did he want to know what she'd been thinking?

"I wasn't staring at your hands, if that's what you're insinuating. And why would that make me smile?" The direction of their conversation alarmed her. Warning bells went off in her mind, telling her she had entered dangerous territory. Something as innocent as closely sitting alone in the apartment together, suddenly took on major importance. Exploring the subject of their physical differences further fascinated her, but heading into that unknown territory spelled danger. Danger to their friendship. Danger to Marta's carefully planned future.

"Did I say you were looking at my hands? You know, Marta, you're not making a lot of sense. You must be tired from your long day. Let's call it a night. You go over things we discussed tonight, and tomorrow over breakfast, I'll give you a little quiz."

Relieved, Marta stood and gathered the papers, dropping several to the floor. "I think you're right, Josh. Thanks for all your help." She scooped up the brochures she'd dropped, replaced them in her folder and made a quick exit. Josh had said she wasn't making any sense. Boy, he didn't know the half of it. Nothing made any sense to her right now. Especially the continual fluttering sensation in her stomach. Her jangled nerves would disappear after she successfully settled into her new position.

***

Struggling to hold onto the grocery sack without dropping it, Marta let herself into the apartment. Today was special, and the occasion warranted a celebratory meal. Today marked the two-week anniversary at her new job. A job that exceeded all her expectations. The customers seemed to like her. She'd been treated with respect by everyone from the boss on down.

In fact, Bill, the owner of the agency had taken her to lunch twice this week. He'd said it was compensation for a job well done. The first time he'd asked her to lunch she'd been uncomfortable. After all, he was her employer. And wouldn't his wife object? Then she'd discretely asked a co-worker and learned he'd been widowed for several years. He and his wife had never had children and he'd spent the last few years building his business and actively participating in several civic organizations.

Marta could tell Bill found her attractive and the difference in their ages didn't prevent them from enjoying each other's company. Surprisingly, their budding friendship hadn't set off any jealous undertones from other the female staff members. Life just couldn't be any better than it was right now.

Marta removed a package of steaks from the grocery bag and placed them in the refrigerator. She'd stick them under the broiler as soon as Josh and Ginger got home. Ginger had returned to work and got around capably using only one crutch to balance with.

Marta scrubbed the outside of the huge baking potatoes she'd bought, covered them in foil and placed them in the pre-heated oven. Just as she started putting a green salad together, she heard the click of the front door. Josh was home. Her heart skipped a beat. She couldn't wait to tell him all about her day.

CHAPTER TWELVE

"You'd darn well better find out where they're going, Rick." Josh slammed the phone book down on the table, knocking one of Ginger's stuffed animals onto the floor in the process. "You told me you'd keep an eye on her. Any moron would know that meant cluing me in on the fact Marta's going on a date with a stranger who's old enough to be her father." Josh paced back and forth with the phone to his ear, listening to Rick's worthless excuses.

He stopped in his tracks. "No way am I going to tell her not to go. Don't you know anything about women? That would be a sure-fire way to guarantee she'd go out with him." Josh ran his fingers through his hair. He wanted to reach through the phone and throttle Rick for not protecting Marta. He never would have let her take that job clear over in Bellevue if Rick hadn't promised to call him periodically and report how things were going. And had he done it? Heck no. Not only had he failed to keep Josh informed, he'd evidently blundered big-time by not paying attention to what went on right under his nose. If Josh hadn't overheard Marta telling Ginny about her date, he'd still be in the dark.

"I know you've got your own job. But how much time would it have taken to stop by her desk and chat with her a little. Or talk with her at lunch. You do eat lunch don't you?" Josh paced faster. However, constantly hampered by the short telephone cord, he could only take a few steps in either direction. "What? They've been going out to lunch together? Every day this week?" Josh felt the heat rising in his face. His blood pressure must have jumped fifty points. How had things gotten so far out of control?

Josh took in a bucket size gulp of air. It wouldn't do any good to blow his stack. He listened to Rick's promise that he'd find out the name of the restaurant and call him back. Grinding out one last warning to Rick, he hung up the phone. Josh rubbed his stomach and headed to the bathroom to find something to calm the pain. He probably had a full-blown ulcer by now.

Rummaging through the medicine cabinet netted nothing but a few personal hygiene products and a couple of expired prescriptions. He picked one off the shelf and read the label. Ginger's pain medication . . . left over from what she'd brought home from the hospital. His scanned the other shelves. Nothing with Marta's name on it. If she were taking birth control pills, would she keep them in here? Shame filled him. There was no reason to believe the worst. Marta wouldn't be sleeping around. He sat on the edge of the tub and put his head in his hands. What would Marta think if she caught him trying to invade her privacy? He'd lose her friendship for sure.

He should have seen this coming. Naturally Marta would make new friends. And inevitably, some guy would find her attractive and ask her out. Had he secretly hoped she'd work there a couple of weeks, and then discover she didn't like it after all? Darn right. Hope, yes. But had he expected it? Not if he was realistic. The question now was, how could he continue to protect her? He'd have to think of something. Only eight hours remained until her date with the geriatric letch she worked for.

***

Marta slipped into the ladies room, grateful for the luxurious carpeting and mirrors in the lounge adjacent to the area where the toilets and sinks were. The garment bag containing her evening dress and shoes hung behind the door where she'd left it when she'd arrived that morning. Bill had told her they had reservations for dinner at a fancy restaurant overlooking the city. The view from the top floor of the Seattle office building was rumored to be spectacular. Afterward, he was taking her to a musical in one of the downtown theaters.

Marta quickly stepped out of her daytime suit and hung it in the bag. The evening promised to be very pleasant. Bill

141

had proven to be a wonderful escort. He knew all the nicest places, and best of all, he treated her like a lady. She'd grown fond of him in the few short weeks she'd worked in his agency. Plainly, he enjoyed her company immensely. Marta slipped the knee-length gown over her head. Bill would love this dress. He always lavished compliments on her and made her feel very desirable. How many women could say that? One last look in the mirror and she headed out to meet her date.

Bill stood next to his new silver sedan, a smile on his handsome face, and a single long-stemmed red rose in his hand. "You sweep me off my feet." Marta accepted the flower and allowed him to seat her. Some women would have insisted on opening and closing their own doors, but she loved being pampered. Bill always made her feel special. She turned toward him as he expertly steered his car out of the parking lot. His immaculately groomed hair was nearly steel gray. However, the color only enhanced his good looks. Some men were like that. They just got better with age. Josh would be the same way.

Marta felt a small twinge of guilt for not telling Josh about her date tonight, but he would've only worried and fretted . . . not to mention lectured her for an hour about the evils of Seattle men. She chuckled, remembering his warning to her just that morning. He'd reminded her to avoid talking to any strangers on the bus.

"You sound happy this evening, my dear." Bill gave her a quick smile and then turned his attention to turning onto the I-90 freeway to head across the Lake Washington Floating Bridge.

"I'm totally content." Or she would be if Josh would stop intruding on her thoughts. She'd bet her next paycheck Josh wasn't thinking of her at that moment. He'd be too busy wolfing down the dinner she'd prepared ahead of time for him and Ginger. Would Ginger follow the written instructions Marta had left? If the casserole didn't bake long enough, or Ginger didn't turn the oven temperature high

142

enough, the cheese wouldn't melt and brown and their meal would be ruined. It was bad enough they would have to eat macaroni and cheese while Marta dined on European cuisine.

Bill's soothing voice broke into her thoughts. "I really should teach you to drive. You'd love the way this machine handles. Besides, if you sell any more cars before the sales force gets a shot at our customers, I'll be giving you a floor model to show, and for driving back and forth to work."

"Josh said he'd teach me to drive." Marta clamped her teeth together. Couldn't she get through an evening without him intruding on the conversation? They hadn't even arrived at the restaurant yet.

"I think it's wonderful your girlfriend's brother is willing to help you out. But has he ever driven a vehicle with this much horsepower?"

"Of course he has." Bill didn't sound like he thought Josh was wonderful. In fact, he sounded a little jealous. Not that it was up to her to rush to Josh's defense. She just didn't like to hear anyone judged unfairly.

"We can discuss it more, later."

"Of course. It's so kind of you to offer."

"Kindness has nothing to do with it. I've made no secret of how much I enjoy spending time with you. In fact, I'd like to spend even more time with you . . . taking you places, showing you the city. I've even thought it would be fun if you learned how to play golf. There are some wonderful links around here."

Bill's comments came as no surprise. He was unlike younger men, who didn't know what they wanted, or worse yet, knew what they wanted but persisted in playing games. Bill wanted her. She knew that without a doubt. He would tell her soon, too. Maybe tonight. He wasn't the kind of man who beat around the bush, or who would string her along and then dump her. No. Bill had marriage on his mind; everything he did for her suggested it.

Why couldn't she muster up a little more enthusiasm? After all, Bill had every single attribute she'd wished for. He was successful, wealthy, settled, considerate, and he doted on her. She'd be nuts to turn her back on man with all those qualifications. Besides she was genuinely fond of him. It had just happened much sooner than she expected, that's all.

A rainstorm, accompanied by high winds, pounded the city as Marta and Bill neared their destination. The city's street lamps illuminated little but the corners they stood on. Few people were visible on the sidewalks, having taken refuge in the few businesses open during evening hours. The dark setting made Marta feel suddenly lonely. She sighed in relief when they pulled up in front of a building with valet parking. At least she wouldn't get drenched walking from the car to the front door. She waited for Bill to come around and open the door for her.

As soon as they entered the building, Marta sensed it was a place where they catered to and pampered the rich. Bill gently placed his hand at the hollow of her back, guiding her toward the bank of elevators. Uniformed employees unobtrusively stood everywhere, just waiting for any indication a patron might want or need anything. Soft lights and soft music compensated for the traffic noise outside. This was a place where the wealthy came to forget about the rest of the world.

A hostess greeted them in a hushed, deferential tone.

Obviously Bill ate here often enough to be known by name. A man in a tuxedo seated them. Marta sighed and sank into the plushly upholstered chair. A discreet glance around the room revealed fresh flowers everywhere. In fact she hadn't seen so many expensive floral arrangements since Mona's funeral.

Across the crisp white linen tablecloth sat her supremely handsome date. This moment had dominated her dreams for years and it was finally here. Her roaming gaze locked on a familiar figure which disappeared behind a column on the far side of the room. Yes, the evening would be perfect if she only wouldn't imagine seeing Josh everywhere she looked. She turned her attention back to her escort.

"You look positively beautiful tonight, Marta." Bill reached across the table, taking her hand. Marta shivered slightly when he raised it and placed his lips on her upturned palm. He treated her like a princess. She hoped he hadn't detected any calluses left from her days of working at the apartments. Not that she was ashamed, or trying to hide anything. Bill knew all about her background and didn't hold it against her. He appreciated the woman she had become. But visible bumps and scars reminded Marta of leaner times.

She regarded him with affection. "Bill, I thought I'd never meet a man like you. I'm so lucky to be your date tonight."

Bill kissed the tips of her fingers, then gently released her hand. "I'm the lucky one. When I lost my wife, I gave up hope I'd ever be content again. In the years since, I've never found another woman I wanted to make happy. For the-Oh, here comes our waiter. I'll finish what I want to say to you after we've ordered."

Butterflies the size of pigeons fluttered in Marta's stomach as she quickly lowered her eyes to study her menu. This was it. This night would mark a major turning point in her life. Her breathing quickened as she contemplated the implications of what she knew Bill would say to her during dinner. She'd planned for this for so long. She knew she could make Bill happy. And she'd have the security and respect she'd always wanted. But wasn't it much too soon? Could she make a decision like this without giving it more thought? If she turned Bill down, would there be any more chances for her?

Marta scrutinized the menu again. Concentrating on making a selection was proving difficult.

"Might I make a suggestion?" The waiter at Marta's side hovered, offering his assistance.

The hair on the back of Marta's neck prickled causing her to pause and look toward Bill. He looked back, smiling and patiently waiting for her to make up her mind. He looked normal. But something was amiss. Even the small hairs on her arms were standing up.

"Perhaps the lady would like the macaroni and cheese?"

Marta's jerked her head around to face the waiter. Josh! What was he doing here? Was he moonlighting . . . trying to earn extra money for the apartments? Josh. She searched his face for an answer, but it was expressionless. What kind of game was he playing? Suddenly wary, she decided to play along till she figured out what he was up to.

"That sounds just fine," Marta responded, not fully aware of what she'd agreed to.

Bill's chuckle caused her to wrench her gaze away from the bogus waiter. "I think our waiter is just having a little fun. I'm sure that's not even on the menu."

Of course not, but it was on the menu at home which Josh undoubtedly knew. Did Josh think mentioning the casserole she'd left would make her feel guilty about eating in a place like this? If he were standing closer, she'd kick him. She couldn't very well do that though. Bill didn't know who he was. He didn't know Josh was a sneak who'd come here to spy on her and her date. Who did Josh Morton think he was fooling?

Marta sat straighter and deliberately took her time reading the menu. She'd order the most expensive item on it. Bill could afford it. Unfortunately the restaurant hadn't printed the prices on her menu. The good news was, they'd written it in English, as well as in French. "I'd like the Specialty of the House, please."

Josh bowed slightly. "Very well, ma'am." He turned and looked at Bill expectantly.

Bill handed his menu to Josh. "I'll have the same. And please bring us each a Caesar salad to start."

Marta narrowed her eyes at Josh while Bill told him what kind of wine to bring. She had to admit he looked stunning in a tux. Josh tilted his head and turned to leave their table.

"Wait."

"Is there something else you wanted, dear?"

"Yes, ma'am?" Both men spoke at the same time. Marta's eyes stayed on Josh. She admired the snug fit of the tuxedo jacket. *Goodness, he looked fine.*

"Aren't you going to write it down?"

"Ma'am?"

"Our order. Won't you forget what we've ordered?"

Josh leaned toward her and spoke just barely above a whisper. "There's not much chance of forgetting, ma'am. You're my only customer." He turned and left before seeing the red creeping up to her hairline.

"Now, where were we?" Bob's baritone voice sounded far away.

"Hum?"

"I was telling you how much I adore you." Bill took her hand again, this time covering it with both of his hands. "Marta. I know I'm much older than you, but I sense we're kindred spirits and our years on earth don't matter."

Marta nodded her head, not trusting herself to find the right words. *My, but it's warm.* She fanned her face with the fingers of her free hand.

"I don't see any point in beating around the bush. We've known each other long enough to know if there's a future for us."

Marta increased the tempo of her fanning. "I-" The cloying smells of flowers and scented candles were so distracting. "I agree, Bill. We're both adults, after all."

"I hope you feel the same for me as I feel for you." Bill removed one hand from the hold he had on her and reached into his pocket.

Josh suddenly loomed into view, pushing a cart conveying an ice bucket and wine bottle. Marta jerked back to avoid his flourishes with a towel and glasses, and in the process yanked her hand away from Bill's.

"Maybe this should wait until after dinner," Bill suggested in a low tone.

Agreeing, Marta nodded her head. She wouldn't have been able to give Bill her full attention anyway. Josh's attempts at removing the cork from the wine bottle were fascinating, to say the least. If she didn't know better, she'd suspect he was using the stubborn cork as an excuse for hanging around. However, no smile graced his lips; not even a twitch in the corner of his mouth. Josh wasn't having a good time. Marta almost felt sorry for him.

A loud pop accompanied Josh's announcement. "There. I've got it." He sloshed some of the rose liquid into a glass and set it down in front of Bill. One of Bill's eyebrows threatened to disappear into his hairline. Had he noticed how inept Josh was at waitering? A giggle escaped from Martha's lips before she could stop it. She took a deep breath and kept her eyes on Bill to avoid another outburst.

Bill sipped his wine, much too polite to make a scene. "Very good. Please pour a glass for my companion."

Marta gripped her hands around a linen napkin. She had to keep a straight face. It was too late to tell Bill the identity of their waiter. What would she do? Make introductions? Bill would wonder why she hadn't said something right away. Josh obviously had no wish officially to meet her date. Yet, if he weren't interested, would he be standing across the room glaring?

"You know, we've never danced together." Bill stood at her side, holding out his hand. When had he gotten up from his chair and when had the music started? He led her to the small dance floor, holding her just close enough so she could feel his every breath on her forehead. Marta clamped her teeth tightly together. This was supposed to have been the most romantic night of her life. Instead it had turned out as . . . as what? Confusion swirled around her head like the nearby couples on the dance floor. She didn't know how she was supposed to feel, but it wasn't like this. Gratitude filled her when the music stopped and they could return to their table.

Nobody had ever had such an attentive escort. Solicitous, tender, charming were all adjectives describing Bill. Had Josh noticed? Maybe he could take some lessons. His image crossed her mind and Josh immediately appeared at her elbow with her salad. *Is he going to be hovering all evening? Why doesn't he just sit with us?*

Josh lunged toward her plate with a giant pepper mill just as Marta reached for her wine. In her frantic attempt to avoid a collision, she jerked her hand back, spilling wine and flipping the salad plate upside down on her lap. A shriek escaped from her mouth before she remembered how to act like a lady. Jumping up, she slapped Josh's hands away as he attempted to wipe the mess off her dress with a soggy napkin.

"You idiot." She screeched at Josh who insincerely mumbled an apology. "You call yourself a waiter?"

"Sweetheart, calm down. I'll buy you a new dress." Bill rose and came around the table. "Let me get you to the ladies room where an attendant can help you."

"No. I'll get there alone. Just leave me be." Tears of humiliation rolled down her face as she made her way through tables full of startled customers. *Darn him, anyway. That was no accident.* She stormed into the restroom, flicking lettuce off her skirt as she went. A sympathetic attendant helped her off with her dress and handed her a robe to wear. The wine had seeped through her dress, dampening her slip. She rubbed at it with a soft terry towel. Was Bill speaking with the manager while he waited for her? Would Josh be fired? It would serve him right. She'd see to it herself.

Marta accepted the hastily cleaned and dried dress from the attendant and put it on. She had freshened her make up while waiting and was ready to storm out to confront Josh. If he still worked there. Her mind focused with steely intent, she swung the door open and emerged from the ladies room. Strong hands grabbed her by the arms and she found herself being whisked down a hallway.

"Josh," Marta exclaimed. "Fancy meeting you here." She pulled her arm back and took a swing at him.

Josh caught her fist in midair. "Shhh. Settle down. I only came back here to apologize."

"Apologize? Would that be for ruining my dress? Or ruining my evening? Or just plain ruining my life?" Marta struggled to free herself from his grip.

"I came here to keep you from making a horrible mistake."

"The only mistake I've made is not running as far away from you as possible the day I met you. Now let me go. Bill is waiting for me."

"No. Not till I've had my say."

"You've said enough. I'm going back out there and telling my date I'm accepting his proposal."

"No. You can't do that."

"And why not?" Marta tussled some more, trying to get Josh to release her.

"This is why." Josh pulled her into his chest and covered her lips with a grinding kiss.

Startled and unaccountably afraid, she stiffened in his embrace. He only held her tighter, placing even more pressure against her trembling mouth. She stopped fighting, not having the emotional strength to escape. New sensations filled her in places she'd never had sensations before. The waves of pleasure from his kiss nearly paralyzed her.

Josh must have sensed the change; he raised his head from her lips and gazed deep into her very soul. She didn't know how to answer the question in the dark blue depths of his eyes. She only knew his embrace was the most dangerous thing she'd ever encountered. Marta closed her eyes to shut out his probing examination. Too late, she realized that doing so intensified the physical sensation of the feel of his kiss lingering on her lips. Her treasonous heart ignored every practical caution her brain sent it. Her mouth accepted his kiss like a flower craving sunshine.

Without loosening his hold, Josh moved her till her back touched the hallway wall. Marta was vaguely aware of voices of two people passing by, but discretion had lost its importance the moment Josh's lips had met hers. She mentally fought to gain her equilibrium, thinking how a diver must feel when forcing his way to the ocean's surface. This wasn't right. These feelings for Josh could ruin everything she'd worked for.

Suddenly Josh's grip relaxed and he pushed away from her. "Tell me. Tell me again you want to go back to your date." His voice, husky and ragged, could barely be heard above the music coming from an invisible sound system. The soft "whish" of the door as two people exited the restroom next to them, momentarily distracted Marta from her thoughts. She refused to meet his gaze, instead, turned her head to look at a place over his shoulder.

Josh's hands moved up her arms to grip her just below the shoulders. He gave her an imperceptible shake. "Answer me, darn it. I love you. I know you have feelings for me. You couldn't have kissed me back like that if you didn't. You've got to stop this foolishness and come home with me." His voice cracked. "Please."

Josh loved her? Did he know the risks associated with that? She could make Bill happy. A marriage to Bill would be easy, like a business deal, a contract. A marriage built on those principles would not fail. Josh wouldn't settle for that. Josh would want it all . . . her body, her mind, and her unfailing blind devotion. Marta's vision blurred. She'd grown to care too much for Josh to ever hurt him.

"Marta. Look at me. I know what you must be thinking . . . that I only view you as a hired hand, somebody to feed me and make me happy. I'd be lying if I said I didn't appreciate all those things. But Marta, I need more than that. I need you. As a partner. A wife."

Oh, God. Help me. Why is this happening now? Marta sucked in a shredded breath. *I didn't know . . . I never thought . . .* Her throat constricted, and she thought she would faint from lack of oxygen. Totally stunned, she couldn't force the words out to answer his question.

Josh let go and abruptly dropped his arms to his sides. "I guess I know the answer. You don't have to say it."

Marta strained to see his face through her tears, but he was gone. He'd left as suddenly as he'd appeared moments earlier.

After a quick detour back to the restroom to splash cold water on her face, she returned to the table where Bill waited.

CHAPTER THIRTEEN

Josh carried a box of his clothes up the stairs to the vacant apartment in building number four. He'd live there till Marta moved away. He'd managed to move most of his stuff the night before when he'd arrived home from his foray into the world of the rich and famous. What a laugh. He couldn't wait to return the tux to the rental place. The sooner he could put the entire degrading incident behind him, the better.

He kicked the door closed behind him. The rest of his stuff would have to wait till Marta left for work. He didn't care to see her this morning. With luck, he could avoid her till she went to live with her white-haired wealthy prince charming.

His stomach growled, reminding him he'd hurried away without breakfast. There'd been no dinner the night before either. He'd gone as far as heating up the casserole, but after one bite, he'd scraped the whole thing into the garbage. Ginger hadn't been home, so he'd had nobody to talk to. He guessed he'd better get used to it. As soon as his sister located her dream man, she'd probably desert him too. He'd end up a lonely, bitter old man, spending his nights and weekends watching TV in his underwear and drinking beer.

Too bad the donut shop didn't make deliveries. The pain in his gut had little to do with being hungry however. Plus, if he wanted breakfast, he'd have to chance running into Marta when he went for his truck. Not that she'd laugh at him. No, she was too kind. She'd probably look at him with pity. Pat him on the head and tell him they'd always be friends. Yeah, right. Friends. They had so much in common. Josh snorted. If he hadn't done some emergency remodeling work last year for the head chef at that fancy restaurant, they probably wouldn't even have let him in. As it was, Sam had been forced to practically beg him to allow him to play waiter.

Josh peeked out the window. Had she left yet? He knew she was awake and dressed by now. He'd heard her rustling around in her room this morning. She'd feel it was necessary to force a confrontation. Marta had even knocked on his door when she came in the night before. Late. Very late. The deed was probably done. Her boss had proposed and she'd accepted. Josh didn't need her flashing any twenty carat diamond in his face. He'd already narrowly avoided seeing it at the dinner table. He wasn't stupid. That guy was about to make a big public display right there in the restaurant. Josh hadn't stopped it. He'd only postponed the inevitable. Pain gripped his chest. He missed Marta already.

A pain shot through his stomach again. Louder this time. He rubbed it with the heel of his hand. Maybe he should have answered Marta's knock last night instead of pretending to be asleep. They could have had it out. She could have chastised him for kissing her and for embarrassing her in front of her date. He could have lied and said he was sorry; he was confused and didn't mean any of it. Late night fights between roommates probably happened a lot in this neighborhood. If they'd shouted the roof down, most likely nobody would even have called the police. They would have cleared the air and he'd be eating scrambled eggs right now instead of hiding in a vacant apartment like the coward he was.

Josh took another look out the window. Another overcast gloomy day. It looked as if a rainstorm was imminent. He pulled on his jacket. What had gotten into him? He'd done nothing to be ashamed of. Nobody was going to chase him from his own home. Especially not a gold-digging friend of his sister's. He squared his shoulders and strode from the apartment and down the stairway. As he reached the bottom step, a spray of water hit him with the force of a fire hose. "What the-?" Josh threw his hands in front of his face to protect himself from the stream of ice-cold water.

Marta stood not a half dozen steps away, waving the nozzle of his new pressure washer back and forth across the siding of the building. She wore the blue jumpsuit he'd bought for her the week she'd arrived in Seattle. The one that fit like a glove and now clung to her where she'd managed to douse herself with the hose. His pulse quickened at the sight of her and he had to bite his lip to keep from saying the wrong thing. Just about anything he could say at this point was likely to be wrong. Especially with the unexpected anger boiling in him. Was life just one big conspiracy to torture him with this woman? Couldn't she have gotten on the bus or in a cab or a limousine and left already?

"What do you think you're doing?" he choked out.

Marta turned a dazzling grin on him. "Just what it looks like. I'm using this hose thingy to get all the old paint off before we redo it."

Josh clamped his teeth together so quickly he bit the inside of his mouth. Torture didn't even begin to cover what she was doing to him. Persecution? Tyranny? She excelled at them all. He couldn't take it anymore. "Have you forgotten? You don't work for me anymore."

Marta's smile didn't dim one watt. "I knew you needed help, and since you hadn't hired anyone to take my place yet, I thought I'd slip back into my old job."

Over my dead body. Josh flexed his fingers. No way was she going to hang around driving him crazy again. Not today, not ever. "I can't afford you."

Marta laid the hose on the ground and flipped the switch on the pump to the off position. With the engine off, the sudden quietness made the unsaid things between them roar in comparison. Josh waited while Marta shuffled her feet. The chill from the spraying he'd just received not only reached his bones but wrapped its icy clutches around his heart. He held his breath as Marta took a step toward him.

"I'd be willing to work without a paycheck." She took another small step, which put her well inside his comfort zone.

"What's the matter? Did lover boy fire you?" Josh instantly regretted the cruel words. What if she *had* been fired? She'd be devastated. Is that why she was here? Had her boss seen them kissing in the hallway?

Marta reached out, barely brushing his chest with her fingertips. "No. But you're partially correct. I don't work for Bill anymore. I quit my job."

Josh's muscles tensed. "Did he do anything out of line to you? I'll break his-"

"No Josh. It's nothing like that. Bill is-was a wonderful boss. But I realized I was happier here. He knew it, too, and released me from my commitment there. I know I take a lot for granted when I ask you for my job back. I know I hurt you last night. I wouldn't blame you if you never wanted to see me again."

"You didn't hurt me," Josh lied.

Marta focused her brown eyes directly at him. He could gladly drown in those eyes. "Does that mean you didn't mean those things you said to me last night?"

A story about just kidding around hovered on the tip of Josh's tongue. Where was this conversation going? She wants to stay. He'd let her go once. He couldn't bear to do it again. She came back on her own. Could that possibly mean-?

"Because, Josh, I tried to tell you I love you too. I wanted to tell you so badly, but I choked. I'm sorry. I've been wrong about so many things. I stayed up late last night praying and asking God to forgive me for not trusting Him. How could I have been so blind to what is really important?"

Josh raised his hand slowly, afraid to break the spell of the moment. She loved him? *Loved him?* He reached for her at the same moment she rushed into his arms. "Marta." He dug his fingers in her hair and kissed her face all over. Her mouth, her nose, her eyelids. Josh almost came apart when she kissed him back with equal fervor. "Marta."

"I love you, Josh. I've loved you for ages and didn't even recognize it. You're the finest man I've ever known. And what's more, you've been my best friend." She cleared her throat and her eyes filled with tears. "But most important of all, I love you the way a woman should love a man."

"And I love you, but we can't be roommates anymore."

"But why?"

"Because we're going to be husband and wife . . . just as soon as we can set a date." He rubbed his lips against hers and pulled her close to him till he could feel her heart beat against his.

The sound of boisterous applause caused Marta and Josh to break apart. Ginger, Miss Treymore, and the people from the tenants' association stood there with wide grins on their faces. "It's about time," they chorused nearly in unison.

Josh clutched Marta's hand in his, refusing to surrender it for even a moment. "Looks like we'll have to finish this conversation in private." He waved to the crowd and pulled Marta up the steps to the vacant apartment. She gave him no resistance.

###